The Love of
My other Life

The Love of My other Life

TRACI L. SLATTON

parvati
press

This book is a work of fiction. Names, characters, places and incidents are either the product of the author's imagination or are used fictitiously. Any resemblance to actual persons, living or dead, or to actual events or locales is entirely coincidental.

Cover and text design by Drew Stevens, studiodrew.net
Front cover photograph: 123rf.com

Published by Parvati Press
www.parvatipress.com
Visit the author website:
www.tracilslatton.com

Library of Congress Control Number: 2013900210
ISBN:
978-1-942523-08-6 (Paperback)
978-0-9846726-3-9 (eBook)
Version 2017-3-13

Books by Traci L. Slatton
www.tracilslatton.com

IMMORTAL

BROKEN

THE YEAR OF LOVING

FALLEN

COLD LIGHT

FAR SHORE

BLOOD SKY

THE BOTTICELLI AFFAIR

DANCING IN THE TABERNACLE *(poetry)*

PIERCING TIME & SPACE

THE ART OF LIFE

with Sabin Howard

To three women who are the loves of many lives

Countess Michelle Czernin von und zu Chudenitz und Morzin

Dr. Jan Bröberg Carter

Dr. Lori Handelman

1 In which insanity enters

I launched myself into a glorious spring day in Manhattan with my customary enthusiasm for leaping over obstacles. I envisioned myself radiating Impressionist pastels as I bounded over everything in my way, every petty detail and wearying obligation, every false cultural ideal and precious lost illusion and brain-fart screw-up, everything keeping me from my ideal life of fame and success and the undying love of my soul mate.

In this case, it was my building super, José, hosing down the sidewalk. "Tessa, we have to talk," he called. "The co-op board is serious!"

"Late for work," I hollered, gripping my bag tighter so I didn't have to pause.

"We have to talk," he insisted.

"Sure," I yelled. But I didn't want to deal with the co-op board. I wanted to relish my own rebirth.

I was painting again! And wasn't it a miracle? It almost brought back my lost faith in something better, something beautiful. To have my talent back, stirring itself like an acorn quickening under the soil. To be returning to myself after a long travail through a dark wood in what I hoped wasn't yet the middle of my life. I was only thirty-four years old, and I hoped to live to at least ninety-seven—painting the whole time. My descendants, if I was lucky enough to reproduce, could pull a No. 6 flat red sable out of my cold, dead fingers when I passed on.

"You'd be better off robbing a bank," José continued, yelling louder as I sprinted away. "You haven't paid your maintenance bills since your husband left three years ago. The board's not going to wait forever!"

"I'll get the money," I screamed over my shoulder before rounding the turn onto Riverside Drive where we couldn't see each other. "Somehow," I panted. The heel of my shoe wobbled, so I stopped by a tree ringed in purple tulips. The contrast of leathery brown trunk and translucent petals pulled me into a reverie.

A landscape painting with purples and browns and sky blues, but almost no reds. A vanishing point far in the distance, as in the vague, exquisite place where ripples fade out in a pond . . .

Someone sighed softly. It was more of a whimper, really. It punctured my moment.

I jumped and looked up.

Not five feet away stood a scruffy man in a beat-up leather jacket. His knee poked through a hole in his jeans, and he wore mismatched sneakers without socks. He gazed at me with an expression of awe.

Homeless. *There but for the grace of God go I.* Then I winced because, if I didn't scrounge up a big chunk of money for the co-op board soon, that would be me. But now I was painting again, and where there was creativity, there was hope. I could soon be selling my landscape paintings for a hundred thousand dollars each. I walked over to the ragged guy. I had only a few dollars in my purse, but I could spare the cash. After all, I could eat the free bagels and cream cheese I knew they had at the Church, and this guy needed a hot meal more than I did.

"Here you go, sir. Buy yourself a cup of coffee." I held out the bills.

He didn't answer. He was intent on my face. His pupils were huge and black. Was he on drugs or just bat-crap crazy? Poor slob.

I picked up his hand and placed the bills on his palm, closing his fingers over them.

He glanced down. "I'll buy you a cup, Tessa!"

Poor fellow—"Wait, how do you know my name?"

I asked cautiously, edging back a few steps. I should have flinched, but I didn't. That should have been my first clue.

"I'm Brian Tennyson," he said. He beamed at me.

He was about my age and not half-bad looking with a smile on his face, if you like the shaggy, unkempt look.

I almost smiled back before remembering that I shouldn't encourage him. How did he know my name? It should have scared me, shocked me at the very least, but it didn't.What was wrong with me? Other than what was usually wrong with me, I mean.

He placed his hand on my shoulder and said earnestly, "I need a place to stay for a few days. Ofee said I could stay with you."

"Ofee?" I puzzled. He knew Ofee? How so? Had I met this Brian with Ofee sometime?

"Isn't he your best friend? He is where I come from. Since you guys were in grade school." The man stepped closer to me.

"Yes, of course I know Ofee," I murmured, scrutinizing Brian's face. Nope, I hadn't met him with Ofee. I would remember that.

"Some things don't change. I just knew you two would be close here, too."

"Ofee's in Thailand teaching a yoga retreat. Uh, how do you know him? And what do you mean, 'he is where you come from'?" I shrugged his hand off my shoulder, but really, I wasn't perturbed. I should have been, but I wasn't. It was as if I knew him through a glass darkly, even though I didn't know him at all.

"That's a complicated question, and I need to ask, what do you understand about decoherence theory?" His eyes widened hugely, like owl eyes. A determined expression scrolled over his face, and he stepped to within a few inches of me. Too close.

"Personal boundaries," I said patiently but firmly, the way I did with the old folks in the eldercare program where I work part-time. Sometimes they sidle inside my comfort zone, usually to hear me better or because time is different for them, and therefore, space is too. I had learned how to re-establish the space without hurting their feelings.

I didn't want to hurt Brian's feelings, either—for no reason that I understood.

Brian didn't say anything for a moment, nor did he move. Then his face lit up. He threw his arms around me and exclaimed, "Love has no boundaries!"

"Let me go," I ordered, struggling.

"Never," he swore. He clutched me tighter. For a guy living on the street and eating who knows what, he was ungodly strong. Then I caught a whiff of something acrid, like sweat and scorched electrical wires and the must of old cellars. I struggled for real.

"I don't care what Ofee told you. Find somewhere else to stay. Bye!"

"But it's only for five days, four hours, and twenty-two minutes, then I'll be gone," he said, gripping me ferociously.

I froze. Fighting wasn't going to solve the problem, I figured that out. What worked with my old folks? Distraction. "Look, a purple chicken drinking vodka while playing an organ!"

"That I gotta see," he said, turning to look. His arms loosened—so fragile is our hold on everything.

I raced away, not understanding how precious was the moment. Isn't it always that way? You don't understand until it's lost.

2 Long ago and far away, in another galaxy altogether

B*rian paced in the front of the classroom as stu*dents filed in. It was his first day teaching this course, Calculus 101—math gut for English majors. It was his first day teaching any course, in fact.

Thanks to an early gift in physics, he was an assistant professor in the physics department. He was also a sophomore majoring in American Studies. The tricky ambiguity of it all meant that he hadn't asked to teach and hadn't wanted to. Yale had thrust it upon him. Some palace revolt among his fellow Yalies, who were always complaining about something. Apparently, the other undergrads felt that the prevalence of non-native English speakers in the lower-level math courses discouraged students from pursuing upper-level math courses.

A young woman with long hair and a shapely form scooted into the back row. Brian straightened. He had noticed her before. His eyes picked her out wherever she was on campus, in front of Linsly Chit or by Commons or outside Branford, which seemed to be her residential college. Brian turned to Rajiv, his assistant, for whom English was an excellent third language. They exchanged a look of appreciation.

Some things exceeded language. In Brian's mind, those things were physics, baseball, and the shapely girl he hadn't stopped thinking about since he first saw her at Freshman Orientation last year.

What transcendental stroke of luck had ushered her into his classroom? Of all the math classes in all the campuses in all the towns in all the world, she walks into his . . . . It reinforced his certainty of the innate goodness of the universe.

The seats in the class were about as filled as they were going to get. "Welcome to calculus, which doesn't have to be boring," Brian said.

A bald guy with three piercings in one ear and four in the other leaned forward. "Aren't you in my Am Stud class?"

"Yep. I'm a sophomore," Brian said. "I'm also a junior associate professor in the physics department."

That got their attention. Indeed, thirty-seven sets of eyes narrowed and focused on him like laser lines of light. Yalies were nothing if not competitive, boola boola. They wanted to know if there really was some-one smart enough to be their professor while also being their peer. Brian let their questions quiver in the same dilemma that any angstrom of light faced: wave or particle? *Let them wonder*, he decided. He picked up a baseball from the lectern and tossed it to Rajiv.

Rajiv dropped the ball awkwardly, then bent and picked it up.

"Rajiv, my teaching assistant," Brian introduced with a wave. He motioned for Rajiv to throw the ball back to him.

With hesitation and a haphazard fling, Rajiv did so.

Brian tossed the ball to Rajiv again; this time Rajiv almost caught it. Brian pitched once more slowly, underhand. "I'm Brian Tennyson."

"Why are you teaching calculus, Brian Tennyson," asked a tall girl with a hatchet face, very black eyeliner, and a short, tight skirt. She had to be a philosophy major.

"So I can play baseball," Brian said. He wound up and pitched a fastball to Rajiv.

Rajiv cringed and fell off the platform. The ball bounced off the wall, leaving a divot in the wood paneling.

The girl with black eyeliner shagged the ball and threw it to Brian. She had a good arm. *She's getting an A*, Brian decided.

"I was an early physics PhD at MIT. Then I came here to major in Am Stud so I can play baseball. I'm teaching calculus because I have to," Brian said. "Someone circulated a petition demanding that math professors speak good English. The petition claimed that non-English speaking math lecturers of all genders, sexual preferences, religious creeds, and races were turning students off math." He paused, grinning. "Yalies are equal opportunity critics, you know." He cleared his throat and took an officious stance, then spoke in a clipped accent. "The administration of this institution takes student needs very seriously."

People smiled. Tension in the class ratcheted down a notch. The shapely girl in back twirled her hair, looking bored. *How can I get her attention?* he asked himself.

The answer was simple and came to him like a flash of lightning over the steppes, as did all his intuitions about quantum chromodynamics. It was always about the transmission of forces. And what force governed all Yalies?

The force for good grades, known as the universal grubbing force.

"Here's the deal," Brian said. "No matter how much you all suck at calculus, no one gets less than a B+."

The class cheered. The girl in back sat up. She had a good smile, soft and full of promise, as Brian had imagined she would. Dazzling, really.

Shazam, Brian thought, looking into her eyes. "Extra credit for visiting during office hours."

3 Of dogs, chocolates, and monkeys flying kites in our universe

I left the loco homeless guy behind. Then I heard the determined patter of rubber soles slapping on pavement. I glanced back over my shoulder. There he was, gaining on me. Sure was a speedy sucker. I accelerated–which one should never do when looking backward–and encountered a force that exploded me into a tangle of ropes and barking dogs.

It was a dogwalker, and he was grunting and rubbing the lump on his forehead where I had banged into him. He was shepherding at least a dozen animals, shifting their leashes around in his hands and muttering about how unsafe the Upper West Side had become. "You're worse than the bicycle delivery guys!" he barked.

Now that was just mean.

But I had slammed into him at full tilt. "Sorry!" I whirled around, trying to disentangle. The more I thrashed, the more the leashes tightened up on my legs. Suddenly, I was upended, legs in the air over my head, my messenger bag flopping away and disgorging all its contents: drawing pad, Vosges chocolates for Mrs. Leibowitz, lipsticks, tampons, receipts from Pearl Paint on Canal Street.

Brian reached through the tangle of leashes and righted me.

"My skirt!" I swore as I beheld a tear in the fabric. "I can't go home and change. I have to get to work." Mostly, I didn't want to have to run back and forth by José again. José was like the enforcer for the co-op board, and they were none too happy with me.

"Your skirt's better with that slit up the side," Brian said, admiringly. "You've got great legs! Wow. I'd forgotten!" He grinned and dodged out of the way to retrieve the drawing pad and box of chocolates.

I scrambled for the lipstick and unmentionables. "This is bad. This is very bad. This is my good skirt. Oh no."

"It's just an article of clothing. It's replaceable," Brian said, popping a truffle into his mouth. "You drew this? It's amazing!"

Okay, so he had fine aesthetic taste. I had to allow myself a modicum of thaw, it was only fair to acknowledge his compliment. "Thank you." I fixed him with a steady gaze. Why did he look so familiar when I knew I'd never met him? Why wasn't I more creeped out by him? I should be. Even if he complimented my drawing.

"I didn't know you were such an accomplished draughtsman."

"I'm a better painter," I said. "Used to be. Am again, since this week."

"You're no acrobat," said the disgruntled dog-walker. He stomped away, shaking his head.

Brian ignored him. "The people are so alive and joyful at their picnic." Gazing intently at my handiwork, he helped himself to another truffle.

"They're not having a picnic," I said. What the hell was he talking about? Didn't he have eyes? I needed to get rid of him. "Give that to me. Stop eating those, they're for Mrs. Leibowitz."

Brian looped his arm around me. "I didn't know you had this kind of talent, Tessa. You must be famous."

Not yet, but someday. Soon. Now that I was painting again, anything was possible. "I'm too busy taking care of old people to be famous. But someday my art will be well known, it'll inspire and uplift people, and I'll be known as the new Turner." Wait, was he trying to look down my shirt? "Ugh, stop that! I have to get to work."

"I'm not looking down your shirt," Brian said,

as if reading my mind. He narrowed his eyes at my jacket, then reached over to straighten it. "You have dog hair all over yourself." He brushed his hands over my chest—hey, was he copping a feel?

"Stop that!" I said, slapping his hands. "Get away from me." Somehow, in some weird way I couldn't explain, I wasn't offended. I was amused. I felt a distant twang of nostalgia.

Maybe I should be on medication?

"I came here specially to see you," Brian said with some urgency. "My time is limited. I only have five days, four hours, well, now it's about three hours and thirty-seven minutes."

"Why do you keep telling me about such a specific amount of time?" I wondered aloud.

"I told you, it's decoherence—"

But I had to stop humoring him. I couldn't explain why my instincts liked him, when my rational mind was screaming at me to shake him loose. But, for once, I had to pay attention to the voice of reason. "Look, a monkey flying a kite!" I exclaimed, as if in wonderment. In addition to being a talented artist, I am an accomplished liar.

Brian turned to look.

I raced away.

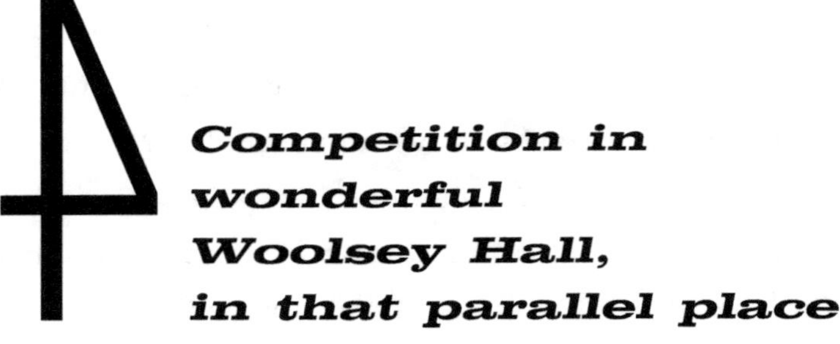

Competition in wonderful Woolsey Hall, in that parallel place

A *large poster in the rotunda advertised: A NIGHT* OF MUSIC WITH YALE MUSICIANS. Waiting to enter, a crowd muttered and stamped at the doors to the magnificent auditorium with its Grecian-themed murals, white columns, and high, vaulted ceilings. Brian, wearing a Red Sox shirt, held a program and pointed to a name printed on it.

"Look, Rajiv, Tessa Barnum," Brian said, reverently. "She plays the cello. She's talented *and* beautiful. And smart."

"Everyone at Yale is smart." Rajiv craned his neck to look over Brian's shoulder. In a heavily accented voice, he said, "She doesn't know you exist."

"Minor detail."

"Rama is in the details," Rajiv observed in a sympathetic tone.

"I like the way her eyes get all soft sometimes.

What is she thinking about? It's not diffy Q's," Brian murmured.

"That's because you're not teaching diffy Q's," Rajiv said.

"I'm going to ask her out."

"Bri, man, she's got a boyfriend from home."

Brian grinned. "I have to apply inertial force and remove his gravitational influence from her frame of reference. I'm researching her so that I have leverage."

"Gravity isn't yet part of the quantum scenario," Rajiv offered.

"That's because gravity isn't a force, it's a warping of space-time." Brian would have elaborated, but the doors opened and people streamed in to find seats. Brian and Rajiv hustled their way into the fifth row, center.

Rajiv spied a square-jawed guy with perfect hair taking a seat in the third row. The guy was chatting a little too amiably with a girl with slicked-back hair, heavy black eyeliner, and a diaphanous shirt with a plunging neckline that arrowed between black-painted nipples.

"That is him," Rajiv said. "The guy with Debbie Doll. She's the woman in our class with the arm like Yogi Berra."

"His name is David Mills, and he drove down from Dartmouth," Brian said. He scanned David coolly. "What's he doing with Debbie Doll?"

"They say Debbie Doll doesn't wear underwear," Rajiv said with a look of supreme curiosity.

"Yogi Berra was a catcher. And a Yankee. What did I tell you about the Yankees?"

"We don't like the Yankees."

"I don't like David Mills," Brian said.

"He's hot, you have to admit. Look at him," Rajiv said.

"He's trying too hard. He looks like Dudley Do-Right." Brian would have expounded on the principle but the lights dimmed.

A man in a tux walked onstage and gestured for quiet. He made the appropriate opening remarks about the musical talent at Yale and then introduced the opening choir performance. After the choir removed themselves from the stage in an orderly fashion, stage hands bustled about, clearing a space and setting up a more intimate diorama, four chairs with a cello and a viola.

Out walked a string quartet that included Tessa. Her hair fell around her shoulders in a magical, shimmering sheet and she wore a slinky-but-classy, strapless black dress that dropped low on her back.

The guy sitting in front of them gurgled. "I can see the crack of her ass! Is that a heart tattoo?"

Brian leaned forward and tapped the guy's shoulder. "Excuse me, that's my future wife. Keep your eyes in their sockets. If you want to keep them."

David, sitting one row in front of the gurgling guy, heard and swiveled around in his seat. He locked eyes with Brian.

Brian nodded slowly. "Game on."

5 Do not go gently; dance, dance into that good night

I was panting and bedraggled as I let myself into the little office inside Collegiate Church where I practice eldercare, and for which I sometimes even get paid. I paused in the foyer beside a poster I had painted: RETIREE DANCE FRIDAY 7:00 PM, WITH BINGO! An artfully rendered bingo board graced one corner of the sign, and waltzing white-haired people entwined in each other's arms enlivened the other corners.

I had painted them after my most favorite charges: Mr. Woolstein, caneless, with his leonine mane of white hair, holding Mrs. Leibowitz in his arms and twirling her over the floor. I imagined that they had cherished a secret, unconsummated flame for each other during their decades long lives, both of them remaining faithful to their marriages while a private tenderness lay dormant, a seed not ready to shoot forth tendrils. Now in the third acts of their lives, they were emancipated into their new, old love.

Come to think of it, was it this very poster that had broken the impasse, that had unlocked the block that prevented me from painting for the last few years, since David had left me? Perhaps. Other signs advertised Bible study, youth groups, and homeless breakfasts, but they were crudely finished. They were not in the same league as my dance poster.

My dance poster was almost real art.

My boss, Reverend Thomas Pincek, swept past me. “Tessa, welcome, welcome. We have a full house waiting for you today. You’re such an angel, you’re packing them in!”

“Thanks, Rev,” I said. “Sorry I’m late. Where’s Mrs. Leibowitz? She was feeling under the weather last week. I want to make sure she’s okay.”

The rev pursed his lips. “Don’t know. Stop by her apartment later if you like. Mr. James here isn’t getting his meals-on-wheels. I told him you would fix him up!” Reverend Pincek clapped hunched-over Mr. James on the back.

Mr. James, who was more than ninety and exuberantly decrepit, coughed and nearly fell over.

But the rev didn’t notice; he was already bustling away to solve twenty other problems for his flock.

I helped Mr. James reconfigure into his walker. "C'mon back to my office, Mr. James. We'll call for you. You look sprightly today, are you working out? Is that a six-pack beneath your cardigan?" I poked my finger at an oblong moth-hole in his faded blue sweater.

Mr. James, whose mind was still as sharp as a scalpel even as his body degraded around it, cackled joyously. "I do one-armed pushups so I won't lose my girlish figure."

Then we were laughing together as I guided him through the pews, where were seated a crowd of waiting old folk, toward the tiny, cramped office in back with my desk and a couple of metal folding chairs.

Mr. James coughed—his emphysema was acting up today—but he beamed at me with bright eyes and a big, gummy smile. I was reminded of why I stay in this job for which I was never trained and get paid too little to pay my rent. No matter how much I've screwed up my life, no matter what I've lost and where I am in my creative process, I always feel uplifted by the appreciation of life the elderly so often display.

Reverend Pincek careened to my door with his secretary and two volunteers in tow. "Only two hours, Tessa. Tithes are down and we don't want to take advantage of you. We can only pay you for two hours."

"I'm here to help, Rev. Money's not my main priority." But even as the words were emerging from my mouth, I had a flash of myself as a homeless person. *I was wearing Mr. James' ragged sweater and standing beside Brian. . . .* I smacked my head.

The rev was speaking, which helped me tear myself away from the image. He said, "Right now, it's ours. I'm praying for some earthly angel to make a big donation, else we'll lose some of our social programs. There's a lot at risk: the soup kitchen, Harlem outreach. Even eldercare."

• • •

Reverend Pincek's words still rang in my ears three and a half hours later as I exited the church and closed the door behind me. I'd solved Mr. James' meals-on-wheels problem, helped Mrs. Anders with her Medicare forms, set up a Gmail account for Mr. Blonstein so he could email his grandson, negotiated with a pharmacy for regular delivery of Mrs. Vaccaro's medications, called the building super to fix the leaky faucet for Mr. Jelonek, and left messages for the respective doctors of Mrs. Altendorf,

Mrs. Crane, Mr. King, and Mrs. O'Reilly. I'd tried to phone Mrs. Leibowitz, but there was no answer.

What would they all do without me?

"I have to help Reverend Pincek," I said aloud. How to do that . . .

"I can't wait for someday when I'm America's J. M. W. Turner. I'll sell my paintings for millions of dollars and donate 50 percent of it to the programs here." I could envision it so clearly: *I'm at an elegant art opening. I'm the star artist, of course. Adoring art lovers swoon at my landscapes, which float, beatified, in a haze of golden light on the walls.*

It was so real to me—I could have been standing in the spotlight of that swanky gallery that even smelled, vetiver-like, of class and money. *I'm wearing a black silk sheath gown.* I'd better start running again so my ass is in shape. *My ass is a whole size smaller.* I love my imagination! *Everyone loves me. I've finally left my past far behind; maybe it's even a charming anecdote to tell my new husband, who wouldn't leave when I screw up. No, he'd thoughtfully, compassionately, lovingly, help me right my career. I even pay my co-op bills. Great art redeems everything.*

Then the lusciousness of it all fractured around me. Someone had barreled into me and was saying my name.

"Brian," I spat. "What's going on? Are you stalking me?"

"Yes. No! I just want to explain." He stepped too close again.

Damned if I didn't get a flash of a UFO whirling through the blue sky. "About your spaceship?" I asked, and it wasn't my kindest tone of voice, though I do, as a sacred rule, try to be kind.

"Decohering device," Brian said, earnestly.

"Listen, Brian, you have to take a hint. I don't know you, and you have to leave me alone."

"The decohering device will return me to my universe," Brian said, as if I hadn't spoken. He grinned ruefully. "My molecular resonance isn't synced to here. It'll decay. It'll dissolve into a pool of submolecular slime."

"Sub-molecular slime?" I slid away from him. Where did he get this stuff? "Are you on drugs?" That would explain a lot—though not my subliminal ease with him.

"Drugs? Never!" He looked offended and then grimaced. "Well, there was that one time at a Blue Oyster Cult concert . . . "

"See ya," I said and turned to hightail it.

"Wait!" he grabbed my arm. "Don't you have a faint sense, a vague feeling, that we've met before?"

"Nope," I lied, warily.

"You must," he said. "Because reality is non-local, and once two particles have interacted, they're forever intimately connected in some way."

"I'm not a particle, and I have no idea what you're talking about."

"I know, it all sounds very technical. I'm a physics professor."

Enough was enough. "Let me go, Professor!" I barked. I know, I'm a pansy, but I can drum up a really nasty voice when I need to. Brian kind of jumped. I fled and ran around the building.

Brian was already waiting on the other side. Was he possibly in two places at once?

No, he was just fleet of foot, faster than me!

I skittered off at an angle. Picking up speed, I flew toward Broadway, threw myself into a crowd of pedestrians, and then descended into the 72nd Street subway station. A train was pulling up to the platform, and I just made it through the turnstile and into the train. I didn't see him. Relief.

6

Of Pablo Casals and the birthmark

Cello music spilled forth from Brian's beat-up boom box. Rajiv sat on Brian's desk because the office was only large enough for a desk with its own chair and another chair beside it for visiting students. Brian crumpled up quiz papers and tossed them to Rajiv, who shot them toward the wastebasket. Despite the three foot distance, Rajiv missed every time.

"Is this all we can listen to?" Rajiv asked.

"Yes, until she comes to my office, hears it, and is impressed with me." Brian picked up another quiz, smooshed it into a ball, and lofted it to Rajiv.

"She may never come to your office."

"She'll come. She's a Yalie, and by definition, all Yalies are grade grubbers."

"True," Rajiv said, missing another shot. The pile of papers beside the trash can got larger and more unruly.

"Also, Rajiv, there is my unifying theory of everything."

"You solved that?" Rajiv yodeled, falling onto Brian and gripping his collar.

"Not that theory of everything, the Brian Tennyson theory of everything," Brian wrested Rajiv off his shirt. "That is, the fundamental axiom that there's good at the root of everything."

"Good at the root of everything? The Vedas say the entire universe is pervaded by God."

"God? I don't know. It's less personal than that. More neutral. Like Heisenberg's uncertainty principle. It's just a statement of nature's intrinsic inscrutability; it has nothing to do with the ability of experimenters to find a particle's position and momentum. It's not a commentary. It just is."

"Heisenberg went out for a drive to get cat food for Schrödinger, and he was stopped by a traffic cop. 'Sir, do you know how fast you were going?' asked the cop. 'No, but I know where I am,' Heisenberg said." Rajiv looked triumphant.

Brian grinned but wasn't distracted by Rajiv's joke. "Relying on the universal goodness, I, very elegantly, set the conditions for her to come in: I offered extra credit for visiting during office hours. She knows her quiz wasn't good so she'll come. When she comes, she'll hear the music. She'll fall in love with me, and we'll get married and live happily ever after."

"Good luck with that," Rajiv said.

A knock sounded at the door. Tessa poked her head in.

Rajiv fell off Brian's desk onto the crumpled papers.

"Oh, you're busy," Tessa said.

"Not at all, come in," Brian said. He waved her in and then kicked Rajiv.

Rajiv whimpered and limped to the door.

Tessa eyed the flotsam and jetsam tide of paper on the floor. "Are those our quizzes?"

"Everyone got a B+," Brian said.

"Except Debbie Doll, who got an A," Rajiv said from the door.

"Is that because she shows her boobs around campus or because she understands the material?" Tessa asked. She sat and twisted around in her seat to hang her backpack off the chair. The side lace of her black thong panties peeked above her jeans.

Rajiv's eyes widened with appreciation. With two hands, he outlined a figure eight in the air, the universal sign for the beloved female form.

"Tell your TA that's sexual harassment," Tessa said.

"Debbie knows the material," Brian said hastily.

He kicked the door shut in Rajiv's face. Then he fiddled with the boom box as if to lower the volume. All the while he gazed adoringly at Tessa.

"Pablo Casals?"

"The great Catalan cellist and conductor?" Brian cleared his throat. "Famed for his recording of the Bach cello suites. You did a nice job with the saraband the other night."

"Think so?" Tessa's eyes softened and filled with light.

"Absotively, posilutely!" Brian exclaimed, feeling himself dazzled again.

"I don't know, I think I drifted a little," Tessa said, but her smile warmed him. "It didn't quite have the power and lilt I was going for."

"Gorgeous," Brian assured her. "I had no idea you were so talented." He paused to pointedly catch her gaze. "What brings you to my office?"

"Bonus points. How many do I get for coming?"

"Half a grade, at least. You'll need the boost, too. That quiz indicated that you don't grok the material."

"'Grok'? Is that from *Star Trek*?" Tessa teased. "You probably know the episode and season, right?" She held up her hand in a distinctive hand motion. "Live long and prosper."

"Right genre, wrong work. But your technique is

impressive." Brian shrugged. He crumpled another quiz and shot it toward the trash can. He missed.

"Baseball is your genre," Tessa observed. "I hear you play first base." Her voice affected a casual tone, but Brian could see a sparkle in her eyes.

"You heard that, huh? Are you asking around about me?" Brian arched his eyebrow.

"Well, you know, people talk," Tessa said, eyelids drooping.

Score! Brian tossed another quiz at the garbage. "Glad I have the chance to play here. I was never good at basketball, but I practice shooting hoops. Never give up, right?"

"Sometimes it's wiser to accept what you can't change. How long do I have to stay to get the points?"

"Are you interested in learning the material?" Brian said. He leaned toward her, so she had to look at him again. "I could actually teach it to you."

"Is it really necessary?" Tessa mimed a yawn. "I'm fulfilling a distribution requirement. I'm not much for math. I'm never going to use it."

"I'd rather be teaching physics. Or better yet, working on my research. But this was part of the deal. Anyway, you're a musician, and music has the elegance and precision of math." Brian wadded up another quiz, shot, and missed again.

"Too much backspin, Prof. Good thing you're not a pitcher. Can I go now? I have a rehearsal. We're playing again at Woolsey next week."

"I'll be there," Brian said in a steely tone.

"Because you're a Casals aficionado?" Tessa's lips quirked, and her expression was knowing.

"I will be by then."

"I just bet you will," Tessa said. She twisted and rose to retrieve her backpack. Her delicious lacy knickers rode up while her jeans drooped, revealing a heart-shaped strawberry pink birthmark on her sacrum.

Brian's eyes gleamed. "Want to go to Naples for a slice sometime?"

"Aren't I already getting an A?" Tessa asked in a reasonable tone of voice. "You know you want to give me one."

"Have a slice with me and you'll get an A+."

Tessa paused with her hand on the door knob. "I'm no math and physics genius who got a PhD at age seventeen from MIT while matriculating at Buckingham Brown, and then came to Yale to major in American Studies and play baseball, but even I know you can't go higher than 4-point-0, Prof. Hey, have you heard that entropy isn't what it used to be?" She threw a wink over her shoulder and opened the door.

Rajiv leaned inward with his ear where the door had been and pitched forward into the office.

Tessa made a sound of disgust, stepped over Rajiv, and stomped off.

"Four kids and a white picket fence!" Brian sang. He could see his whole bright future stretching ahead of him, starring Tessa, and it was beautiful, the ultimate proof of goodness inhabiting the known universe.

7 Real originals and other forgeries

It was a typical Chelsea gallery, which meant I was sorely tempted to burn it to the ground. This could be considered not arson but public service.

José's warning about the co-op board had put me in mind of finding a gallery to show my landscapes. Now that I was painting again, and because a few years had elapsed since everything imploded, I was ready to go out into the world with my work once more. Maybe. Almost.

But this was the wrong gallery. It was filled with Damien Hirst knockoffs and Jeff Koons wannabes. I looked at some tags and my ire bubbled up: everything was outrageously overpriced. If I sold even ONE of my beautiful landscape paintings, at a fraction of these prices, I could fund Reverend Pincek's programs for a year. Two, and I'd be out of trouble with the co-op board.

It had a personal hook too since I'd run afoul of

the art world three years ago. I'd labored diligently for years to master my craft and it had all gone up in a plume of betrayal, rumor, and false accusation.

"So much money for so little talent," I was murmuring. I was triggered, and I couldn't uncouple myself from the steam engine of my bitterness. "I paint better than this. I have to show my work. I have to get out into the world, so people know they have options, they don't have to put up with this drek."

Then I froze. An entire wall was covered with Picassoesque female nudes that were duplicated in checkerboard after Warhol. It was trite-*cum*-gimmicky, with a soupçon of cheesy, and I knew it well. Too well, all too well.

My heart almost stopped beating in my chest when I saw the price on the label.

Why did the bad art command these prices?

Why wasn't good art recognized and valued?

Why did people rush to believe hearsay and refuse to hear the truth?

An elegant, bearded man in a hot-pink suit approached. "I'm Frances Gates, the proprietor of this fine establishment. How do you like these original Cliff Bucknells?"

"Original?" I squeaked. There was nothing original at all about Cliff Bucknell. I knew that first hand.

"Of course, they're original. I heard about the big scandal a few years ago, but those rumors were just a marketing ploy, I can assure you. Only Cliff Bucknell has a genius this masterfully droll."

"Masterful," I repeated, not breathing at all. The volcano inside me was building up pressure.

"Come this way, darling, I have something that will really take your breath away." He ushered me toward a small grinning skull covered with rhinestones and colored sequins. "Cliff Bucknell's rendering of Damien Hirst's *For the Love of God*. Isn't it witty?"

The numbers on the placard swam in my vision and made the room flicker around me. "It's. It's. It's a million dollars?"

"There are those, and I am one, who think it's better than Hirst's!" Gates placed his hand on his chest.

"But, but . . ." I squeaked, as my throat closed and my past erupted, molten hot and viscous. Why had I ever thought I could elude it?

Was there no way for me to rectify it?

"I can see how moved you are," Gates said with a sympathetic nod. "Listen, we're having an opening of Bucknell's work, his first show in years." He leaned toward me, to whisper directly into my ear. "His first show since that scandal, which was completely false, you understand. Here's an invitation." He placed a gaudily-printed postcard in my hand.

"Oh God," I gurgled. The postcard slipped to the ground as I threw my hands up into the air.

"Darling, do you need help?"

"No, but these artists do!" I cried. I couldn't help it. I was so appalled.

Gates recoiled. "I show the finest post-modern art in the city!

"You do? So where is it? The finest post-modern art in the city. Where is it?"

Gates gestured with his hands like an orchestra conductor. "What do you think all this is?"

"What do I *think* it is? Or what do I *know* it is?" I grabbed his sleeve and dragged him to a tank in which floated a cubit-zirconia encrusted thighbone. Price: $300,000. "This is expensive merchandise. Expensive, ugly, meaningless merchandise. The mercenaries who made it ought to be shot in the kneecaps!"

Gates shrugged out of my grip. "If you're one of those people who—"

"One of those people who loves *real* art?" I demanded. In my mind, I stood in the Vatican beneath Michelangelo's sublime *Creation of Adam* on the ceiling of the Sistine Chapel. *Magnificent and awe-inspiring, God reached out his hand to his cre-*

ation Adam, and a symphonic chorus of Alleluia's played . . . .

But my mouth was still moving as if it were a car without a driver careening down the highway. That happened to me sometimes when I was taken over by the bright, fierce spirit who lived within though was mostly occluded. "One of those people who loves the kind of art that uplifts and ennobles people? The kind of art that sees you through your darkest hours and inspires you? One of those people?"

"That's so archaeological," sniffed Gates. His words punctured my happy Renaissance bubble.

I stood, once again, in Chelsea, in a gallery filled with tawdry baubles that some sneering, condescending, punitive, mentally challenged art demi-god had deemed worth hundreds of thousands of dollars. "There's nothing archaeological about beauty."

"If you want beauty, take a taxi to the Met. I thought you admired Cliff Bucknell; you had such an obvious emotional response to his work." Gates looked wounded.

"Cliff Bucknell is a has-been fraud," I said.

That pushed Gates over the edge. He turned on his heel and flounced off.

I trailed him. I heard a noise behind me as someone came in, but I didn't turn my head to look. I was too intent on reaching Gates, on somehow making him understand what he, the art community, and the world at large needed to know: that art isn't about irony and wit and commercialism and fashionableness and all that superficial glamour that means nothing and goes nowhere fast. Art is about something deeper, more real. Something transcendental that shows us the way to our better, truer selves. Art is about beauty. Art is about meaning.

The meaning to which art inspires us is worth drastic action.

Gates was mincing rapidly away. I grabbed his arm and yanked him around to look at some ghastly purple still lifes. I said, passionately, "People only buy this stuff because it matches their curtains!"

"What kind of hair are you shedding?" Gates wondered, staring at my jacket. "You need a new hairdresser."

"Mr. Gates, there are artists who have studied their craft and developed their aesthetic out of a valid tradition and who have something to say that isn't pedestrian!"

Gates held his hand to his forehead and honked. "I'm getting a sinus headache. Is the barometric pressure dropping?"

What the hell, why couldn't he hear me? I grabbed him by the collar and shook him. "You can show meaningful art!"

“Not if I want to make a living,” he responded. He wriggled out of my grasp and closeted himself in his office.

They came in a tidal wave: disgust, anger, sadness—all my old feelings about the silly triviality into which art had degenerated since Marcel Duchamp did us all a disservice and foisted a urinal on us, which had a minute and a half of shock value before the novelty wore off. I mean, it’s been more that a hundred years, and artists, with their lack of originality and creativity, are still doing that urinal. I wandered back to the skull.

Then I couldn’t breath. *What?*

I was ensconced in a bear-hug like an iron corset.

“Like that skull? It’s only a million dollars,” chirped Brian.

“I hate it, and I want it to go die in a hole,” I whispered, struggling and wheezing for air. “Didn’t I tell you to get lost?”

“How do you know you’re a physicist? You avoid stirring your coffee because you don’t want to increase the entropy of the universe,” Brian asked and answered his own joke. Then he chuckled. That’s right, he was crazy.

“How crazy and delusional are you?” I demanded. I froze, and maybe the sudden cessation of motion caused him to release me. I drew in a big sweet lungful of oxygen. I was happy to breathe freely. I was also incomprehensibly glad to see Brian—which really pissed me off.

"What I mean to say is, physicists think for themselves. You can't just tell them what to do. It used to drive you crazy." He picked up the skull and shook it next to his ear. "Alas, poor Yorick. I knew him, Tessa, a fellow of infinite jest."

"Put that down," I hissed and grabbed his arm. "The rhinestones will come off. It's only Elmer's glue."

"Here, didn't you ever want to hold a million bucks in your hand?" Brian thrust the *objet d'art* into my hand.

I gawked. I was overwhelmed by a welter of feelings: disgust, envy, and other, fiercer emotions. I turned it over and over in my hand. "So ugly."

"People love this stuff."

"People who don't know better; they've been duped by the corrupt commercial art establishment to think that the only thing art has to do is hang on the wall and get more expensive!" It was everything that was wrong with the art world, which had cost me so dearly.

"Down, girl," Brian said. He took the skull from me and put it back on its base. "Someone will pay this much for it. A million dollars. Know what I'd do with a million bucks? Take you to Vienna. Mozart's 'hood. You always wanted to go there."

There was no answer to his absurdity, and my own was showing its life-demolishing fangs. I stormed off. Brian followed me. When I looked back, he was gazing at me with a melting expression. I took a deep cleansing breath. "Brian, I keep telling you to go away. Why are you still following me?"

"The thing is," he said, and tilted his head in a bird-like expression of interest, "we're married."

"Professor, if you really are a professor, I feel sorry for you, but—"

"We are husband and wife. In an alternate universe. Lots of them exist. Imagine: there's an alternate world where you love this art, where Cliff Bucknell is your idol."

"Impossible," I scoffed. "Cliff is a loathsome, narcissistic, manipulative, deceitful user."

"No, in this other world, you're obsessed with his work. In your eyes, it's the pinnacle of human artistic achievement. There's a universe where you own it. Maybe there's even a universe where you love it enough to steal it," Brian continued. He opened his hands expansively. "You can't restrain yourself, your passions. The security cameras are out of order, there's no guard and no attendant. So, in that other universe, you make the decision to slip it right into your bag."

“No way.”

“It solves all the problems in your life, to possess this skull, which represents the pinnacle of beauty and wonder in the universe,” Brian said. He made one of his unrestrained gestures that stirred me to some distant, unresolved recognition, like a past life memory that could never be recovered—because I didn’t believe in reincarnation.

“You are out of your mind,” I said, though I suddenly glimpsed a certain logic in his madness. Wouldn’t it just solve a lot of problems if I took the skull? It wouldn’t even be theft, really, for reasons I couldn’t help but remember.

“Nope, just imagining the possibilities. Don’t you do that?”

I glared at him and didn’t answer.

“You have more gumption in my universe,” Brian observed. “Not gumption. Center. Self-possession. Something. You have bark but no bite here.”

“I do not bark, and I do so have bite,” I said, a little archly, truth be told. I mean, I know I’m a pansy, but do I need to have some cuckoo homeless guy pointing that out to me? No. No, I do not need that. Besides, discretion being the more attractive part of valor, being a pansy is part of my ineffable charm. Such as it is.

Of course, it does beg the question of why I haven’t been out on a date in over a year. *I need to start running again and get my ass in shape* . . . . It occurred to me that my imagination, wonderful as it was, was not going to tone my derriere.

I was going to have to take action.

"Nah, I don't think so," Brian was saying. "You seem lost and confused, actually."

"I am not. And this *is* your universe." I marched back to the skull and stared hard at it.

Brian was only a half-step behind me. He cupped my chin to turn my head to face him, then he assumed a lecturing posture and an authoritative tone. "One theory in physics says that every possible outcome happens with 100 percent probability."

I felt myself being stared at and turned my head just fast enough to see Frances Gates peering out of his office door. I waved at him: Please come out! Maybe he could rescue me from Brian's lecture.

Gates slammed his door.

"Damn it. He's afraid of a confrontation with someone who sees art not for its monetary value, but for its quality of moving and uplifting people," I muttered.

"He's afraid of you," Brian said. "That barking thing you do."

"I could do a lot of good with a million dollars."

"See, I've got you thinking about the possibilities, that's a good thing," Brian enthused.

"Oh, I always think about the possibilities," I muttered. "It's the unintended consequences that trip me up."

"You're learning. Now, come with me." He slipped his arm around my shoulders in a friendly fashion.

Did he expect me to go with him back to his flying saucer? Was he actually a psycho serial killer trying to lure me to some private spot where he'd murder me with an axe? Somehow—I didn't know how—I was sure it wasn't because we were married in an alternate universe. I didn't think so. Somehow, I thought he was harmless. Possibly even well meaning. But, to err on the side of caution, I asked, "Come with you where?"

"Back to the big bang. Which wasn't a single event." He leaned his head close to mine and spoke in a conspiratorial voice. "Imagine, if you will, the velvety black of space, with multiple explosions radiating out . . . ."

His tone was so soft and persuasive that I could visualize it perfectly. It would make a lovely painting of some kind, but not a serious one, not high art, no . . . . What the hell was wrong with me? I knew better than to let him draw me into his *mishegaas*.

Brian was still talking. "In the theory of eternal inflation, there are endless, on-going big bangs breaking off from an underlying substrate of inflating space-time. Each one produces its own separate cosmos. Mine, yours."

Out of my peripheral vision, I spied a security guard walking in the front door, carrying a paper cup of deli coffee. This was my chance! "Guard, guard," I called.

The guard trudged over. "Can I help you?"

I shoved Brian at him. "This crazy man is bothering me."

"I'm not crazy, I'm visiting. I know her better than I know my own self," Brian returned vigorously.

"I've never seen him before today," I said.

Brian pointed at my pelvis. "She's got a heart-shaped birthmark on her back, right above the cleft in her ass—show him, Tessa!"

How did he know?

The guard cast his eyes at my ass with prurient interest.

"I'm not pulling down my skirt to show anyone my behind!" I said, outraged. But I was a little spooked. How did this goofball know?

Frances Gates must have summoned a pair of testicles because he marched out of his office, braced as if for battle. He asked coolly, "Is there a problem here?"

"Love that suit, hot damn!" Brian said. He threw

his arms around Gates and hugged him effusively. What was it with that crazy man and hugging?

What was it with that crazy man and his absurd, tantalizing ideas?

"Oof," mumbled Gates. "A simple handshake will do. You're spewing germs all over me."

"I'm Dr. Brian Tennyson, physicist at large," Brian said, pumping Gates's hand. "Where'd you get this? Is it custom? It's awesome. Never felt anything so soft!"

"Isn't it fabulous?" Gates asked, preening. "I'd tell you the top-secret thing they do to the fabric, but then I'd have to shoot you."

"I always wanted a red velvet suit," Brian said.

"There's no time like now," Gates said.

"Ain't that the truth. You always think you have forever, then you find it's over before you realized," said Brian.

The guard jumped into this thoroughly inane conversation, and I took advantage of their masculine absorption in gossip to do what I needed to do, and then to slip away.

My bag was a little bit heavier.

And I felt a new gumption surging through my veins.

8

A kiss by any other name

The lecture hall in Leitner Observatory was filling to capacity. Brian stood near the door, his eyes searching the rows. He saw her finally—in the back row. There was an empty seat beside her and he quickly slid in. He saw a sheet of music spread out on her lap, atop her notebook. He noticed that her hands were small and slim, and the fingers of her left hand bore thick calluses. It made him tingle to think of those fingers on his skin, on his neck and his back.

Then he thought of his hands on her skin, neck, and back, and his whole body burst into flame. He had to let her know how he felt. It was time. She wasn't his student anymore. She was fair game.

"Welcome to astrogut, astronomy for non-science majors, an easy A," he told Tessa in a hoarse voice.

She straightened, and wasn't that a hopeful smile on her face? "Are you teaching this class?"

"Nope," Brian said, looking at her mouth. "I'm stuck in calculus again this semester."

"So what are you doing here?"

"Auditing the class."

"Right," Tessa said. She leaned toward him, a slight motion, but it spoke a near infinite amount to Brian, who had a good grasp on quantification. "I think you're just glad you're not my teacher anymore, and you're here to see me."

"That's true," Brian said. He realized he was barely breathing and forced himself to inhale. "Listen, I have to know: how many kids do you want?"

Tessa's lips curved, and she shifted around in her seat. "Look, Prof, you're cute and all, but I have a longtime boyfriend from home. You and I can only be friends."

Brian tried to think of something quippy and clever to say, something *über*-Yalish and ironic that would impress her. He just didn't have it in him. This was always the problem with language; at crucial moments, it failed. But that's what physics was for. And Brian got physics, understood it all the way from his scalp to his toenails as he had since he was seven years old and picked up his cousin's tenth-grade physics textbook.

There was but one physical response to Tessa's words. Brian went for it. He grabbed her by the shoulders and kissed her, quickly and sweetly. When he released her, the music had fallen off her lap. And he knew what those calluses felt like on his skin. They were much smoother than they looked.

9 Lumpy asses and husbands

I was standing in front of Mrs. Leibowitz's door, knocking and knocking. No one was answering.

Then the door swung open by itself. It hadn't actually been closed.

This wasn't good.

I stepped into the foyer, a small but well-furnished affair with a Persian rug, an old-fashioned crystal teardrop chandelier, and a mahogany case that displayed ceramic figurines. "Hello?" I called. "Mrs. Leibowitz? Hello?"

Still no answer.

I walked through the foyer into the living room. This room had good-quality but threadbare furniture, a couple of bookcases jammed full of old books, a grand piano, and another of those elegant Persian rugs. The air was so still I could see motes of dust swirling in the sunlight pouring in through the window. The stillness made me uneasy. "Mrs. L, are you here? It's Tessa."

Silence.

I made a circuit of the apartment, ending up in her bedroom. I called her name and paced around the room. I paused in front of her credenza to look at the photos: graduations, weddings, babies, family vacations. My fingers slid over a bridge trophy, bronzed baby shoes, and a plaque reading: PTA CHAIR – WITH OUR THANKS. A silver frame engraved with HAPPY 50th ANNIVERSARY showed Mrs. Leibowitz and her smiling husband leaning toward each other.

I picked up the anniversary picture. "Poor Yorick, indeed. Why would anyone pay so much for a resin skull that doesn't reveal any truth about the human condition?" I felt a wispy nostalgia for something I didn't have, and would I ever have it? I had lost a husband and nearly my own soul, and didn't know if it was possible to replace either; there was no guy in my life under the age of seventy-five, and what about children? But I told myself I was just sad about the state of the art market.

It was the way to become an accomplished liar: spend a lifetime practicing on yourself.

With a sigh, I replaced the photo on the credenza, with all the other mementos of a life plentifully lived. I walked back to the kitchen. A small tub of whitefish salad from Zabar's sat out on the counter, opened. A tarnished silver salad fork lay beside it. Why would she leave it that way and go out? She wouldn't. What had happened to her? I felt a flicker of fear.

That's when I noticed the back door was cracked open.

I threw open the back door and peered into a shadowy stairwell. "Mrs. Leibowitz? Are you down there?"

Very faintly, a thready voice answered, "Tessa? Is that you?"

• • •

Fortunately, Mrs. Leibowitz wasn't injured. She'd taken out the trash to the back hallway where her doormen collected it. She thought she saw her neighbor's cat perched precariously on the windowsill, so she climbed down to the landing between floors—whereupon the cat leapt to the stairs and scrambled away. Just watching it made her so tired that she sat down to rest. Then she discovered she couldn't move. She figured someone would come along, so she just waited and hummed and watched the cat watch her from the windowsill of a higher landing.

I mostly carried her back up into her apartment.

I wanted to call her doctor, but she argued with me and begged to be taken outside to enjoy the fine spring air. She pleaded so piteously that I acquiesced, eased her into her wheelchair, and took her down in the elevator. I arranged the lacy shawl over her shoulders and thought how marvelous she was, elderly but beautiful in her bones, her white hair fluffing out around her face.

"I hope you take care of yourself as well as you do me, Tessa," Mrs. Leibowitz said, patting my hand.

"I don't think much about myself, I just want to help, Mrs. L," I told her. "Hey, here's a question, what would *you* do with a million dollars?"

"People often ask a question of others because they're asking it of themselves. So, Tessa, what would you do with a million dollars?"

"Give it to Reverend Pincek, so he can keep his programs going," I said promptly. And wouldn't he be happy? *I could just see him with that big, sunny smile of thanks on his face as he realized that his worries were over and his programs would continue . . . .*

"Nothing at all for yourself? Don't you have needs?" Mrs. L asked gently.

"Oh, I almost forgot, I have something for you." I dug into my purse and pulled out the box of chocolates.

"Such fancy chocolates," Mrs. Leibowitz cooed. "I couldn't."

"You must," I assured her. "Otherwise I'll eat them all myself and get a big lumpy ass, and I'll never find another husband. Even if I have a husband in another life, I won't have one in this life."

Mrs. Leibowitz giggled. "My dear, men like big asses. My Bernie certainly did. That's why our oldest son came only six months after we were married. He was almost ten pounds at birth, too."

I giggled with her at the innuendo. Then the elevator door opened, and I pushed the wheelchair out into hilly Riverside Park, which was green and breezy and full of New Yorkers out to enjoy spring after a cold, snowy winter. Mrs. Leibowitz smiled up into the sun and looked ten minutes younger, and I was suddenly glad that I'd yielded to her and brought her to the park instead of to the doctor. She looked so happy.

I wondered if I would feel that way when I was her age. I wondered if I would feel that way at *my* age. I wondered if I would ever feel that way again or if remorse and regret would follow me around forever, like a little dog begging to be fed. Which reminded me of all the baggage I was carrying.

I asked, "The real question is, what would you do to get a million dollars?"

"Marry rich," Mrs. Leibowitz said promptly. "Actually, marry a good man who'll grow rich with you. That's what I did. We weren't rich, not the way your generation sees wealth, but we were comfortable."

"Marry," I said, and an unexpected surge of energy caused me to burst forward with the wheelchair. Mrs. Leibowitz exclaimed and stretched out her arms. I thought I heard someone behind us and I craned around to see, but there was no one. Was I hearing things today?

My focus returned to Mrs. L. I said, "You were lucky. You had a wonderful marriage and a happy, fulfilling life with Bernie."

"He wasn't my only suitor. Other men liked my big ass."

I had to agree. "It's true. I've seen the pictures, Mrs. L. You were a bombshell. You're still a knockout."

"When I was young, I looked like Greta Garbo. It drew men to me. I chose the one who made me laugh. Not that it was always easy, but we had that to come back to."

"That is good for the long haul," I agreed. I sighed. "I wish I could find a man. I think I'm almost ready. I'd choose a guy who gets it about art. Who makes me feel good." We had reached the crest of a

small hill in Riverside Park. I paused to gaze down toward the Hudson River. With the lemony light and the soft wind stirring pale green buds on gray-black tree branches, I immediately had a flash of a landscape painting: *the river, its gleaming surface, the soft cerulean sky and rolling hills . . . .*

"You'll find someone, Tessa." Mrs. Leibowitz's soft, reedy voice broke my reverie. "A pretty girl like you, so kind, and you have a fine ass, too. You should be proud of it. You should wear tight skirts and show it off more. It's empowering to feel frisky in your clothes and that will attract men."

"After David, I'm, well, I don't want to get my hopes up."

"This isn't about hopes," Mrs. L said slyly. "This is about action. You have to troll for men. How long has it been since you got laid?"

"Mrs. L!" I protested, and dissolved into laughter. There was a reason she was my favorite of all the people who came to the church. I sobered suddenly. How long had it been since I got laid?

I couldn't remember. Had to be David, of course. But when? Those last few months before he left, I was a mess. There wasn't a lot of conjugal nookie happening.

Then I saw something, some movement behind

a tree trunk: a man trying not to be seen. Him! It was Brian, still stalking me. I felt electric with indignation. Boy, was I going to let him have it. I bolted toward him and didn't quite register it as I should have when my messenger bag whacked the wheelchair.

Brian saw me coming. He didn't seem to know what to do, and he broke left, broke right, and then dove for cover.

I took a flying leap and tackled him. "Stop following me!"

"I came here to see you. Ow, that hurts!" Brian struggled in my grasp. "You left the art gallery without saying good-bye—ow!"

"Now do you think I have some bite?" I demanded.

"That expensive piece of art was gone," Brian said. He got his leg around mine and executed some sort of wrestling move, flipping me off him. He sat up and gave me a hard look. "Did you take it, Tessa?"

"That skull is not art," I spat and scrambled to my feet. "It is merchandise. It doesn't do anything whatsoever to enrich humanity, it just lines the pockets of the corrupt dealer system that's hijacked the production of art." I shook my finger at him.

"But it doesn't belong to you," Brian said. He jumped to his feet and shook his finger back at me.

"Someone has to save Reverend Pincek's social welfare programs. You were the one who said I stole it in another universe because it represented all that was good and true."

"That's not what I said, you've taken my words completely out of context–"

"Wheeeeeee!" sang Mrs. Leibowitz.

Brian and I turned. Her wheelchair had inched over the crest of the hill and was slowly, inexorably rolling down the other side, picking up speed until it was whizzing downhill. Mrs. Leibowitz was laughing. Her arms were extended and her shawl whipped around her.

"Oh my God," I cried. Brian and I both charged after her.

For a homeless crazy dude, Brian was in very good shape. He reached the wheelchair first and grabbed it at a run, then slowly, adroitly, turning it away from the oncoming traffic of Riverside Drive, brought it to a stop.

"Nicely done, young man," said Mrs. Leibowitz, whose cheeks looked a little pink. "I thought I'd go for a tumble."

"Inertia, right?" Brian said. "Reminds me of my favorite *Star Trek* joke. Some physicists sent a letter to the show's writers asking, 'How do the inertial dampeners work?'"

"Mrs. Leibowitz, are you okay?" I asked, panting and kneeling down to examine her.

"And the writers wrote back, 'Very well, thank you'!" Brian laughed uproariously.

"I'm fine, Tessa," Mrs. L patted my arm. "Your friend was telling me a joke that I don't get."

"He's not my friend. He's a crazy street person who's leaving," I said. I trotted around behind the wheelchair, so I could discreetly bare my teeth at Brian.

"You seem like friends," Mrs. L said. "You seem connected somehow."

"We're not," I started.

"We really are." Brian cut me off to pump Mrs. L's hand and beam at her. "Dr. Brian Tennyson, nice to meet you, ma'am. You're a great looking lady. Beautiful eyes you have. Wow."

If he hugged her, I'd deck him.

Mrs. Leibowitz giggled and leaned toward Brian, clinging to his hand. "Did you hear, Tessa? He's cute, and he's a doctor."

"Not that kind of doctor," I clarified, making shooing motions at Brian. "He's a physics professor. He claims."

"Absotively posilutely!" Brian said, squeezing Mrs. L's hand. "I specialize in macroscopic decoherence."

“What’s that?” Mrs. L answered, and was she fluttering her lashes at him? Well, well, Mrs. L, you sly girl. Okay, he’s cute, but still.

“Imagine, if you will, the velvety–”

“We’d better get you home, Mrs. L. I want to call your doctor and see why you’ve been feeling so poorly,” I said. I grasped the wheelchair with one hand and slapped at Brian with the other. Then I grabbed his elbow and jerked him over close enough to me, so I could whisper in his ear. “Go away and leave me alone. I mean it.”

“Not until you give back the skull,” he whispered back.

“I’m taking care of Mrs. Leibowitz right now, I’m not thinking about the skull.”

“You have to take care of yourself before you take care of other people. That means giving back the skull, so you don’t go to jail,” Brian whispered furiously.

But Mrs. Leibowitz interrupted our bickering. “I’m getting tired again, Tessa. Better take me home. Brian, it was lovely to meet you.”

• • •

In the end, after speaking to Mrs. L's doctor, over her objections, and passing on to her his stern advice to refill her prescriptions and take them as directed, I elected to leave her building by way of the service door in back. I poked my head out and didn't see Brian, so I tiptoed out and peered around the corner to see him staring at the front entrance. I slithered back out of view and then headed off in the other direction.

10 The paradox of forgiveness

From Mrs. Leibowitz's place, I went to the Collegiate Church. I had in mind that I'd talk to Reverend Pincek, maybe get a little perspective on things. That kooky Brian was causing me some perturbations of the soul.

Blame him, sure; he was an easy target. It wasn't like my life had been in the crapper for the last three years, and I was now at the point of having some decisions made for me.

The choir was practicing, the rev singing with them. His pink cheeks were shiny with good cheer. Indeed, his whole being thrummed with the joy of music and worship. He was so perfectly settled into his right place, and so suited to be where and who he was, that the very air around him evened out into greater harmony. It was as if he radiated a note that brought everything around him into beautiful resonance.

I felt a little envious. Also, suddenly, lonely. Three years ago I had made some terrible choices that resulted in my life breaking up around me, as if it were a behemoth ship hitting an underwater mountain of ice. My budding career as a painter was ruined. No gallery would touch me with a ten-foot pole. Then my husband left, and took with him some core part of me. I had been unable to paint until this week.

But was it really David's fault that I had lived in a frozen psychic time conglomerate for the last three years? That all I had done for so many months was go to work, see Ofee and a few other friends, and then hide out in my apartment, watching reruns on Netflix?

The song ended and the rev swept over to me. "I love that hymn," he said cheerfully. "It reminds me that I don't have to mastermind things, that I can rest in God and trust."

"Trust, what's that?" I joked. I sank down in the pew. "I can't rest when I have to make my life work. I have to take action. Sometimes, you know, you have to do something. Something you never expected to do, something bold and maybe even shocking. But then, how do you know if you did the right thing?"

Reverend Pincek beckoned for me to follow him. He strode through the church.

I was on his heels, but sunbeams streamed through a stained glass window, throwing out rainbow prisms of light and I had a flash: *a painting of the opalescent light.* Very Turner, with a smidgen of the Hudson River Valley, but without the river.

"Did you hear, Tessa?" the rev was asking. He gave me a quizzical look. "It's a paradox. Lao Tzu said, 'Work without doing.'"

I was still a little dazzled by the light. "What if you do something iffy, but you're taking care of someone, or else accomplishing great good? And anyway, it's not what it appears to be on the surface because there are hidden elements at stake?"

The rev picked up a hymnal off his desk. "It's not about accomplishment. It's about a heartfelt vision of your life. You're good at that, Tessa."

"I don't know, I don't have a vision for my life, I make it up as I go along," I murmured, following him back out to the waiting choir. "Then I shock myself and go too far. Maybe that's the problem. I'm already mid-thirties, and I'm still just bumbling along."

"It's not about age," the rev said in his kindly tone. "The Divine is always with you. As *A Course in Miracles* says, 'I no longer need to be the director of the universe, and can simply rest in the assuredness that 'I need do nothing' but be still and let His forgiveness touch my mind.'"

The choir, as a body, gathered around the rev and me—and broke into song. The Alleluia chorus. The rev and I exchanged a smile.

"I could really use forgiveness," I said more somberly than I intended.

The rev, despite his unflagging bonhomie, is really very sensitive. For a moment, he looked stricken, his face melting in on itself like a wax mask. Then his usual placid expression returned. "Not you, Tessa, you're one of our angels. And it's not about sin. That's too literal an understanding. Forgiveness is a much broader concept than that. It has to do with wholeness."

His secretary, Joan, yodeled out from his office. "Reverend, Rabbi Schwartzbaum is on the phone about the peace march!"

"Okay," he called back. He turned back to me. "Tessa, do you need me?"

"Mrs. Leibowitz is failing. Her doctor says she's wearing out with old age. He wants to move her to a hospice. She refuses to go."

"Oh dear, let's call her kids," he said, his brows beetling together on his forehead.

"She doesn't want to worry them. She's adamant about that."

"Hmm. You'll think of something, Tessa, you always do. You've been a blessing and an asset to our eldercare program since the day you started here. What would we do without you? What's it been, five or six years now? You were fresh out of graduate school when you started here. We do appreciate your good work. Hope we can keep you on. Our funds are so depleted." He was already hurrying away to take the cordless phone that Joan was waving at him.

Just like that, I was determined anew that some financial blessing would show up for the rev and all his worthy programs. But I couldn't wait for a radiant, hymn-singing being to wave a magic wand over the situation. Until the angel appeared, there was me.

Screwed up, anything-but-an-angel me, who still had a few resources up her sleeve.

I pulled out my cell phone and found the old contact information.

11

The laboratory at night, or through the rabbit hole

Brian was alone in the lab, as he always was these days. He was thirty-something now, still dressing like a grad student. His shirt was stained with sweat and unevenly buttoned, his hair ragged. His face wore a raw expression as he stared at a strange machine. It resembled an arbor with a tangled flowering of wires, like a spider plant with a hundred babies, all of it connecting to several computers.

It was strange but immeasurably beautiful. It was his last hope.

Brian fingered one of the nodal bursts of cables and ran his hands down along it to a laptop that was bigger than the others. "I wish you were a time machine," he told it. He held his breath, wondering if it would answer.

"Affirmative, Brian. I read you," was what he half-expected to hear. But only silence responded. He smiled bitterly. "If you were a time machine, I could go back and change things. That's what I really want to do. Why didn't I invent that?"

A bustle and the rubbery treading of sneakers sounded. Rajiv entered the lab and leaned against the wall. He was older, too—the same age as Brian. He gave Brian a compassionate look, the look of unvarnished acceptance that passes between old friends who've shared too many beers, career victories and mishaps, conquests, weddings and funerals. "The device jumps laterally into parallel worlds. There's no changing the timeline."

"Yet," Brian said.

Rajiv shook his head. "Bri, man, you must accept the limitations of the physical universe. It's amazing you've come this far. Amazing and terrifying. What you've created goes against the order of the worlds somehow. The entire universe rests on dharma, and what are you doing to dharma with this device? I wonder if it will really work?"

"Only one way to find out," Brian said. His fingers pounded out something on the computer keyboard, then he leapt at the machine and threw some switches. The whole contraption lit up. Brian yelped with excitement, and the hair on his cervical vertebrae tingled. He fiddled with a dial and tapped again on the keyboard.

A soft hum like monks chanting 'om' rose and

filled the lab. The arbor glowed with blue light in concentric rings like the expanding wavelets in a pool.

"My God, Brian," Rajiv yelped.

"Maybe I can change something, somehow," Brian said. He closed his eyes prayerfully, and then stepped into the brilliant blue center of the arbor.

"You're not going to test it on yourself!" Rajiv said. "Brian!"

12 Lamb chops, plasma, and bliss

It was late afternoon by the time I found myself at my front door. After talking to the rev, I'd made a call I never thought I'd make again. So there you have it, Dante was right after all: hell really does ice over.

To comfort myself, I went downtown to Pearl Paints on Canal Street and stocked up on tubes of oil paints. Utrecht makes fine oils, a pleasure to use, with their buttery texture and brilliant color and complex chemically smell. I put down the shopping bag on the floor to rummage around in my messenger bag for my key.

Smoke was pouring out from the bottom of my door.

I found my key finally and jammed it in, but I couldn't get the door to open. In a panic of fear and frustration, I banged my head against the door.

It was a reflexive gesture. I wasn't expecting it to open.

But it did, and there stood Brian, wearing an apron. *My* apron. He sang, "Hi, honey, welcome home."

I had a moment of utter, speechless shock.

"Would you like a drink, Tessa?" he asked. "You look like you could use a drink."

I recovered myself enough to manage a few words. "What, what are you doing here? How'd you get in?"

"The door was unlocked," Brian said.

"No, it wasn't." I tried to push through him to see what was on fire in my home. My brain had short-circuited, but I figured I could put out the fire and then deal with the fact that a crazy homeless man had broken into my apartment.

Brian threw an arm around my waist and halted me. He gestured with his chin at the door on which hung a sign that said NOTICE OF HOUSING COURT. A luminous landscape was painted over it, but the letters still showed through. "Great painting," Brian said. "Almost as good as your figure drawings."

"You broke into my apartment, and you're talking about my paintings?" I asked incredulously. "You, a total stranger?"

"We're not strangers anymore, you met me

today," he said in a reasonable tone. "Did you do that recently? Is that why you said you were painting again? It's really beautiful. Exquisite."

I softened because I couldn't help it. My art was the way into my heart. "Thank you. I was rather pleased with my use of color and the composition of trees framing the stone wall." I stole a look at Brian; I really didn't think he was an axe murderer. Would an axe murderer be able to appreciate my painting?

No, axe murderers would like the ugly crap sold by Frances Gates.

Brian held aloft that professorial index finger. "Notice that this isn't a canvas. It's an eviction notice."

He had no right to be standing in my kitchen. I tore myself out of his grasp. "What's all the smoke?"

"Lamb chops caught on fire. Greasy suckers."

I ran to the oven and threw open the oven door. Inside, smoldering on my cast iron skillet, were blackened, coal-like lumps of meat.

"I can scrape off the charred part," Brian said.

Those were my last frozen chops, and I was saving them for when I was really, really hungry and couldn't stand another bite of free bagels and cream cheese. "No! Get out of my apartment right now. You have no right to be here!" I was yelling and stabbing the air with my finger. A tiny, querulous voice in the back of my being wondered, had I somehow encouraged him today by not being forceful enough with him? Had I been bizarrely tolerant, so that he thought I was inviting him in? “Brian, I mean it. Get out, and don’t bother me any more!”

“But I came all the way from a parallel world to see you, and I only had five days, four hours, twenty two minutes, not a second more, and the clock is counting down.” He made a placating gesture with his hands, palms facing me, trying to appease me.

“I don’t care what crazy farm you escaped from. I don’t know you. I don’t want you in my home. Now. Get out!”

“I’ve got nowhere else to go.”

“I’m calling the police,” I decided. I grabbed the phone and punched in 9-1-1.

“If you call them, I’ll tell them you stole a Cliff Bucknell from the Frances Gates gallery.”

I hung up the phone. I squared off to Brian. Both of us were determined. I could feel the tension like a block of marble between us. “You really think I’m going to let you stay here? A criminally insane derelict? I should whack you in the head with that cast iron skillet and drag you outside to the park where you belong.”

“You’d never do something like that.” He grinned and shook his head. His stance didn’t relent. “You’re a bleeding-heart caretaker without a spine here. In my world—"

"'My world?' There's only one world, you lunatic. One!"

"Nope. You're wrong. There are lots of universes. Parallel worlds, a near infinite number of them, a different world for every decision. We live in an unfathomably enormous multiverse."

"You're from a different universe?"

"That's what I keep telling you. You listen better in my world."

"I'm not a caretaker, I'm a blocked artist with noble ideals for helping humanity—"

Brian made a strangled sound. He gave me a look of total disbelief, as if words had failed him. Then he grabbed me and kissed me.

At first, I fought him, of course. But then something else crept in. Something soft and luscious, something that made me tingle south of my naval and north of my kneecaps. It had just been so damn long since anyone kissed me—and for being a crazy homeless guy with delusions of physics grandeur, Brian could kiss.

And kiss and kiss and kiss.

And kiss some more.

And then I was sort of limp like a pool of uncongealed Jell-O.

Brian lifted his head. "Blocked, noble, et cetera, et cetera? Is that what you say to yourself when you sleep alone, night after night? When's the last time you went on a date? When's the last time a man held you and kissed you until your panties crept up under your armpits and your insides turned to plasma? When's the last time your lover held you all naked and sweaty until you were done moaning and screaming and were limp with bliss?"

"My sex life is none of your business," I said. It came out as kind of a mewl and I would have hated myself, but I was sort of in shock at the masterful way Brian had kissed me. I had never in my life been kissed with such authority. It gave me a whole new regard for him. Not that I'd ever admit to that.

"You don't have a sex life."

"At least I'm not crazy." To sound serious and self-possessed, I said, not meaning it, "Let me go."

"You stole a million dollar piece of art because you think it's ugly, and I'm the crazy one?" He chuckled shortly and then kissed me again. He brought my palm to his lips and kissed my hand gently, intensely. Slowly, expertly, he ran his lips and tongue along my wrist.

All the nerve endings in my body unfurled and sang opera.

"I have to help Reverend Pincek," I murmured. What else could I say? It was as if this stranger knew my body's innermost secrets.

"Sweet, but you have to give it back." He unbuttoned my top button and kissed my clavicle and the hollow of my throat.

I moaned.

"I just want to please you," he said softly.

"It's been so long. Don't stop!" The words poured out of me—I couldn't control them.

Brian stopped kissing me and looked me full in the eyes. "Tessa, sweetheart, are you sure?"

That's when I owned what I wanted, and I didn't need words for that. I kissed him back.

13 Barolo and missing moles

We cuddled under the duvet. Brian's body was as lithe and muscular as his speed and reflexes had promised. And I might be the artist, but the man was a genius with his hands.

And his mouth.

It was as if he'd made love to me a thousand times already, and he knew precisely where, how, and when to stroke, press, and accelerate.

That's right, this is what it was like to get mine. That's right, I have an erotic core. Mrs. Leibowitz was right, it was all about getting laid.

My ex-husband had never managed to stir me to such lush intensity.

I felt like a kitten that had lapped all the cream and I stretched luxuriously. Brian watched me with an inscrutable, though slightly bemused, expression on his face.

"You're good at this!" I said.

"Give me twenty minutes and I'll be good at it again. Maybe ten." He nuzzled me.

We could spend all afternoon in bed . . . . Oh, wait, no we couldn't. "Oh. I have a meeting."

"What kind of meeting?"

"With a guy."

"What kind of guy?" He pushed himself up on one elbow and touched my breast. "Here, you have a red mark on your breast. Where my Tessa had a mole."

"My ex made a comment. I was self-conscious and had it removed. I always had to be perfect for David."

"Good ole Saint David the savior," Brian said bitterly, biting off the words with more savagery than the situation called for. He rose from the bed and slipped on his jeans.

I sat up, wondering at his bitterness and admiring his finely knit body. He was well made, indeed, with beautiful symmetry, perfect proportions, and rounded limbs that fit into his torso and pelvis, as if he'd been designed by Polykleitos, the ancient Greek sculptor. Brian's skin was warm toned like linen cloth with a blush to it. I thought about painting him. Could I get him to model for me during his five days and four hours here? I wondered again what had provoked him. Saint David? As if.

But when Brian turned to face me, zipping his pants, he was composed. “Want some wine? I opened a bottle from the cupboard.”

“There’s no bottle,” I started. Then I remembered. “You opened the last bottle of Barolo from my wedding?”

“Why not?”

“I was saving it for some wonderful occasion, like when I sell my first painting.”

Brian scanned me. “You have all those beautiful landscapes stacked in the living room, and you’ve never sold a painting?”

I shook my head.

“Why not?”

“Maybe because I’ve never shown them.” I flopped back down onto the bed.

“Never ever?” he queried.

I shook my head again.

“Why the hell not?”

I groaned and pulled the cover over my head.

“Okay, we’ll celebrate being alive today.” He shrugged. “What’s more wonderful than that?”

“You know what I mean,” I grumbled, throwing back the blanket. “Fine. I’ll have a glass. But quit going through my stuff.”

He grinned and left the bedroom. I hoped he didn’t notice my messenger bag in the kitchen.

I looked around my bedroom as if seeing it for

the first time: plain white walls with cloudy outlines where paintings used to hang, bookcases with vacant spaces where David's books had sat, picture frames facing down. It was a symphony of deliberate denial.

Maybe I was seeing with new eyes. When my budding art career fell apart and David left, I packed away my landscapes and displaced all the photos, so I didn't have to keep looking at my failures. I kept the room clean, but other than that, I had wasted not a second on it.

Maybe it was time to put back up some paintings. Maybe it was even time to put away some of the photos.

Brian came back in, whistling, and handed me a glass of wine.

"You have a sneaky look on your face," I observed.

"*L'chaim*!" he said, raising his glass.

"Here's to saving eldercare."

"You've got to—"

"Don't tell me to give the skull back," I said, quaffing the wine.

"You stole it."

"It's not theft."

He raised an eyebrow. "Because it's ugly?"

I grunted. "It's insured. There'll be a huge settlement."

"Tessa, please. Frances will call the police, and you will go to jail. He knows you took it."

“He can’t prove it. The security cameras didn’t work. You said so,” I said smugly.

“Not going to fly.”

“What if it was really actually mine, all along?” I challenged him. “What if I could prove it?”

“You took it from the gallery. You have to give it back.”

“That gallery represents everything that is wrong with the contemporary art world that prevents real artists, good artists, from being successful!” I said, passionately. “That gallery should be burned to the ground as a service to humanity!”

“That doesn’t give you the right to take the skull.” Brian shook his head and wandered to the dresser. He pulled up one of the frames. “Why do all your photographs of David face down?”

I buried my head under the pillow. I couldn’t explain any more than I could explain my own responses to Brian, which I knew went up and down like an amusement park car on a rollercoaster. Or maybe I could explain them, and I didn’t want to because then I’d have to face things about myself that I preferred to deny.

I had to get a grip on myself. It was just that for the first time in a long time, I felt alive again. It was like the pins and needles feeling when blood rushed into my foot after I’d been sitting on it for a long time: painful and awkward, so that I'd hop around spastically.

Maybe there was a reason I'd numbed myself.

"Look at him trying too hard. The chiseled face. He's too perfect. I think rakish good looks that flirt with nerdy but, asymptotically, never land there, are more attractive. Don't you?" Brian cut a muscle-man, Mr. Universe pose.

"Anyone who uses the word 'asymptotically' is a nerd, by definition. What does that even mean?"

Brian held up his finger in his lecturing posture. "An asymptote is a line that a curve approaches but never meets."

"I don't speak science lingo. I didn't take science at Columbia."

"You did at Yale, in my universe," he said, his voice and his face softening.

"I went to Columbia to be with David. I was accepted at Yale, but I didn't go. I knew that would be the end of the relationship." I sat up and tucked the sheets around myself. I wished Brian would let go of the whole mythical-other-universe thing. I wasn't sure why he'd attached himself to me, but I was giving him a chance. More than a chance. I'd let him into my bed, which was something I'd never done lightly.

To quote Mrs. Leibowitz, "Wheeeeeee!"

I struggled to regain a semblance of control over my life. Maybe if I found out more about Brian, if I pierced his effusive fantasy life. "If we're married in your mythical world, how do you know David?" I asked. "He wouldn't be part of my life if I went to Yale and got with you."

Brian had crossed over to the window and was looking out into the courtyard. "The guy you're meeting, does this have anything to do with the skull?"

But I wasn't distracted. There were still too many unanswered questions. "If you know Ofee, you know what his name stands for."

Brian glanced back over his shoulder and drew a line across his forehead. "One Fucking Eyebrow."

"Would Bard Rubin have the same nickname in a parallel world? Hmm," I wondered aloud. "Of course, that information is on Facebook."

Brian came back to the foot of the bed and fixed me with what was clearly an inquiring physics professor look. "Your figure drawings have a lot of heart. Why not sell them instead of a stolen piece of art? Or your landscapes. I looked through all the canvases in the living room and in your closet. They're gorgeous. They shouldn't be hidden away."

"You went through my paintings?"

"To get to know you better." Brian pinched my big toe, which stuck out from under the duvet cover. "The you here, in this universe."

"Yes, this universe, that universe. How did you get to this universe?" I asked sweetly.

"I built a decoherence device. It was genius, really. I got the idea when I was ten and watched an episode of *Star Trek*. I filled up a notebook with my ideas. I kept writing them down in notebook after notebook. But the time I was thirty, I had filled a hundred notebooks."

I felt frustrated and I jumped up and pulled on some jeans. What was I thinking, sleeping with this kook? Why wouldn't he just be real with me? Why the elaborate set-up? What was my deal with the bad karma around men? "Cool. I have to go now."

"To the meeting. Right. With a guy to fence the skull? How do *you* know someone like that?"

"I met him through a teacher."

"That doesn't sound like you, the puritanical artist."

"I'm not puritanical," I said, indignant. "I'm idealistic!"

Brian wrapped his arms lightly around me and kissed my shoulder. "Idealists don't steal."

"It's not theft," I insisted. "And I have to help Reverend Pincek."

"You have to help yourself, Tessa. I meant to tell you, your super stopped by before you came home."

I wriggled out of Brian's arms. "Before or after you went through my personal belongings?"

"He thought your painting on the door was beautiful, but they're going to lock you out of your apartment."

"I think I'll have another glass of wine," I decided.

"I don't know how they can do that. Maybe because it's a co-op. You don't actually own your apartment, you own shares in a corporation."

"That's it! Shares in a corporation! That's exactly what I need. Then I can sell them and move to Florence and paint the Duomo. And I can take more figure painting classes at the Florence Academy."

Brian grabbed my head from either side and forced me to meet his gaze, which was serious and saner than could be expected, given his delusions. "Tessa, focus. Fantasies won't help. You need a strategy. You owe years of back maintenance fees."

"I have a strategy," I said. "Sell the Cliff Bucknell abomination."

"Then you're fucked. Because I can't let you do that," Brian said, in a soft, determined voice.

14 Central Park is where whales swim

I was striding along purposefully, clutching my messenger bag. Brian trotted alongside, keeping up. I refused to look at him.

Around us swirled the throngs of Central Park: dogwalkers, teenagers, runners, mothers and nannies pushing strollers, bicyclists in all their gear and attitude, tourists and pedestrians and gawkers and ne'er-do-wells. Day was waning into night, but the colorful masses teemed outdoors, shifting and reforming, a living kaleidoscope.

"I have to sell it now. Don't you understand? I've gone this far. I have a vision for helping Reverend Pincek. I can't back out."

"There's still time for you to do the right thing," Brian said, stubbornly. "You're better than this."

I looked at Brian and thought about fessing up. There was a backstory, and if he knew it, he might look at things differently. His heart was in the right place, even if he was crazy.

But I got distracted, wondering: what does it say about me that I had slept with a crazy guy? Nothing good. Another one of my errors, foibles, mistakes, and blunders. There were so many of them.

But now was not the time to flagellate myself. Nor did I want Brian to expose himself to risk. I said, "The guy I'm meeting is trouble. Serious, big-time trouble. You shouldn't be here. Beam back up to wherever you came from."

"Do you watch *Star Trek* in this world?" Brian asked.

"Is Captain Kirk one of the voices in your head?" I asked, sympathetically. "Oh, there's Rat Rock." I pointed to a whale-like gray outcropping with blue sky spilling out around it. A tall, sinister, Euro-trashy man leaned against the rock and smoked a cigarette.

But I didn't focus on Guy, as I should have. Instead, I had a flash: *Rat Rock in a landscape painting, rugged shades of gray with the arching azure sky and the green park.*

Painting. We weren't far from the Met. "Hey, after this, let's go to the Met!" I suggested. "There's a Raphael exhibit. His use of color and perspective is mind-blowing. It'll quiver your timbers all the way to your soul."

“Raphael, funny.” Brian laughed once, a single ‘ha’ like a bark. “I’m used to hearing you rave about Pablo Casals.”

I’d heard of him. “Isn’t he the one who was asked why he practiced the cello for three hours a day when he was ninety-three, and he said, ‘I’m beginning to notice some improvement’?”

Brian nodded and looked away almost too quickly for me to see his face wring out. I didn’t comment because it was clear he didn’t want me to notice his sudden wrenching expression of sadness.

Besides, business called. I got a little queasy. “That’s him. The guy. Guy.”

“The guy guy?” Brian asked, confused.

“That’s his name, Guy.” I opened my messenger bag. *What?* My stomach fell out of my torso and I rooted around in the bag, growing more frantic by the second. “Where is it? Why isn’t it here?”

“I took it,” Brian said proudly. “I want you to return it.”

“Brian! This guy means business!” I gasped.

But Brian had marched up to Guy and was waving his finger in Guy’s face. “You shouldn’t smoke, mister. Did you know that it’s the leading cause of premature death?”

Guy smiled and exhaled a sooty purple plume of smoke into Brian’s face. “Not in my line of work.”

Guy shifted his leather jacket so Brian could see the switchblade sheathed in his belt.

Yep, it was Guy, all right. Same accent of uncertain origins; was he Russian? Chechen? Albanian? North Dakotan? I hailed him. "Hey, Guy, so here we are."

"Tessa Barnum," Guy said, his face writhing with avarice. "We meet again. Hell must be a winter wonderland. The ancients reasoned this way: as it is in nature, so it must be in art. Therefore, the cold of Hell is resolved into cold, hard cash."

"Ha ha," I said blithely. "You know my flair for the dramatic."

He dragged so deeply on his cigarette that I imagined the alveoli of his lungs blackening and shriveling. That image gave me a burst of pleasure.

"Nice to see you," I said, with a smile that was genuine because it commented on his impending lung cancer.

Guy said, "I was surprised to get your message. It was only the fourth time I was surprised in my life. The number four is a key resolving number. Four are the cardinal points; the principal winds; the seasons; four is the constituent number of the tetrahedron of fire in the *Timaeus*; and four letters make up the name of Adam."

"Yes, um. I was surprised myself."

"Meet *again*?" Brian demanded. "Tessa, how often have you done this? Have you stolen before?"

"Cliff Bucknell, excellent commodity, always a market for it. Such is the dramatic struggle between the beauty of provocation and the beauty of consumption," Guy said.

"It's not beautiful," I said sternly.

Guy shrugged. "Show me."

"The thing is," I started nervously.

"The thing is, she's got to give it back!" Brian exclaimed.

Jeez Louise, did he not understand what was going down? I grabbed Brian by his upper arm and dragged him a few yards away, motioning for Guy to excuse us.

"Tessa, have you lost your friggin' mind?" Brian asked. "What history do you have with this goon?"

"Shh!" I hushed him. "Keep your voice down. It's just, um, stuff with my old teacher. Brian, listen. For real, for once. Guy is dangerous. He cut the thumbs off someone who blew a deal."

"My God, Tessa—"

"This meeting isn't a girl scout reunion, okay? The art market has an ugly side to it. There are plenty of people who don't care about the provenance of a piece, if they want it. They'll pay a lot, wow, a whole lot, to get what they want. Because of that, there's a whole thriving underbelly to the art business."

"You'd never be involved in something like this in my world." Brian was visibly distressed, and he wiped his face with both hands.

"There's art theft, of course, on spec, for resale, or for ransom. There's fraud and forgeries and trafficking. Looting. A hideously ugly side to the business of masterful beauty." I willed him to understand: he could not treat Guy in a cavalier fashion.

"This isn't you, you're not like this."

"In your world, I must be some kind of sanctimonious nun, who won't do what it takes."

He stiffened and glared. "You're my wife, the most amazing woman and friend and musician ever. You're strong and wonderful."

But I had had enough. I didn't want to participate in his hallucinations any more, even if he was the most considerate lover I'd ever taken to bed. Not that I had a large sampling to compare him against because I'd married young, but still. I reached inside myself for the union of patience and firmness, the way I often did at work. "Look, I've been humoring you."

"Humoring me, that's what you call what we did? I knew we should have done it again right away. The decohering slowed me down. Damn!"

I felt my cheeks burn scarlet. "You seem harmless, despite the delusions and fantasies. But this is real. And there's a side to it you don't understand. So please, just shut up and let me work it out, so I can keep my thumbs and go back to painting." I marched back to Guy, steeling myself for a difficult conversation. I could feel Brian's forlorn eyes on me.

15 Like a Virgin

B*rian sat on the floor of Tessa's dorm room in* Branford College. She had a tiny single, which seemed wallpapered and carpeted with sheet music. The cello leaning against her desk made a dissonant contrast with the boom box, which was blasting "Like a Virgin."

"Isospin should be allowed, it's a real word," Brian grumbled. He looked across a scrabble board at Tessa.

"Not in the scrabble dictionary," Tessa said, wagging her finger at him. "You know the rules. Drink!"

"The scrabble dictionary is out-of-date, unfairly biased against scientific terminology, and just plain *wrong*," Brian said. He reached through the pile of empty Pabst Blue Ribbon cans on the floor to find a full can. His woozy fingers curled around one. He pulled off the tab top and then chugged. Then he belched, an elongated sound like a cow lowing.

Tessa fell over, laughing.

"You're gonna win just because I can't spell anymore," Brian said.

"I'm going to win because I'm the superior player."

"In your dreams," Brian returned.

"It's true, I got 800 on the English SAT."

"Show off." Brian sniffed. Then he gave Tessa a serious, brooding look. "What did the male magnet say to the female magnet? From your backside, I found you repulsive. However, seeing you from the front, I find you rather attractive."

"You don't like my backside?" Tessa leapt to her feet, turned, and wiggled her tush at him. Just then, the boom box experienced a moment of quiet. "Justify My Love" kicked up.

"This is the song I first got laid to!" Tessa said. She swayed her hips. She danced rhythmically, seductively, as she sang along with the song–and all the while she stared into Brian's eyes.

"You said we could only be friends, but you don't have to have a PhD to know that's not friendship music."

"'Don't want to be your sister, either, I just wanna be your lover,'" Tessa sang, huskily. Then she ran her tongue over her lips.

Brian grabbed her by the ankles. She tumbled

down, laughing. Brian rolled her onto her back and climbed atop her. "What poor schnook did you date rape to this tune?"

"He loved it," Tessa said, weaving her arms around Brian.

"I bet he did," Brian said. He pressed his lips against hers, softly and quickly.

"My brother's math tutor. He was twenty-three. I was sixteen. I never told anyone, not even David. Kiss me again, Prof."

But Brian paused. "What about old David, Mr. Perfect from back home? I don't want to share you with him."

"That's done," Tessa said. "He wants a girl at school with him. Besides, he was getting boring." She faked a yawn and rolled her eyes.

"Good," Brian said. "Just so you know, I'm telling everyone what we're about to do. Twice."

Tessa laughed. "That's not very gentlemanly of you."

"Yes, it is, because I'm going to marry you, too," Brian said. Then he kissed her for real because he meant it.

16 Picnics are such sweet sorrow

The ugliness that repels us in nature exists, but it becomes acceptable and even pleasurable in the art that expresses and shows beautifully the ugliness of ugliness," Guy said. "I will have that skull." He passed by Brian, blowing dark smoke in his face and sneering in warning.

"I'm not on board with the ugliness of ugliness," I said, but affected my most unctuous manner. "Tomorrow afternoon," I called to Guy's departing back.

Brian was looking dispiritedly at three teenagers bouldering across Rat Rock, cheering each other on. He mused, "Climbers have such fun together. That sport is all about camaraderie. I always wanted to do it."

"You have to give me back the skull before tomorrow," I told him.

"I never got to learn, though. No time, and other

priorities. But I'm glad I spent the time the way I did. I wouldn't change anything."

"Brian, focus!" I snapped. "I need the skull. Seriously!"

He gave me a wan smile, and it was as if most of the fizz had gone out of his internal ginger ale. But as he looked at me, his eyes brightened. "I know. Let's get food and have a picnic, like the people in your drawing."

I snorted. "They're not having a picnic!"

• • •

But a little while later, we were. We sat on a bench along the bike path by the Hudson River boat basin, not far from where Mrs. Leibowitz had gone for her ride. It was evening and the sun slanted down over the river, which reflected back streaks of red, orange, and pink. Across the river rose the variegated Jersey skyline, with tall buildings whose lit windows winked at Manhattan.

I was soon deep in the idea of rendering the whole view as a landscape painting. It would be so breathtaking—I could even give it a Goya-like sadness—it would be beautiful and evocative in the way that nothing at the Frances Gates Gallery even aspired to be. What was wrong with contemporary art that the very principle of beauty had been lost? That ugliness had been enthroned? That art had become so constrained into individual expressiveness that no one but the artist who assembled it knew what it meant?

Didn't people realize that they were shortchanging themselves by accepting this drek as art?

"You know what's weird?" Brian was saying.

"Weird?" I knew damn well what was weird. "Weird is Cliff Bucknell getting millions for crap. Weird is Dung Madonna ever getting funded. Annie Sprinkle, for Chrissakes. The junk that passes for art in the Whitney Biennial, that's weird!" Somehow I had found my way to my feet and was gripping Brian's arms.

"Down, girl. Boy, you get triggered easily by that art stuff. I meant weird in terms of parallel worlds." Brian pried off my fingers and maneuvered me firmly back to my seat beside him on the bench.

"Oh, that. Nothing's weird. It's not weird at all, you showing up like a bad virus and claiming to be from a parallel world. Not weird, nope."

"Ha ha," Brian gave me an ironic, sidelong glance. "What's weird are the differences between here and where I came from. Some are minute. Some are huge. But you're still Tessa, my wife. You are, and yet, you aren't. It's a paradox."

"You're not my husband."

Brian reached over and took my hand gently. "Believe me, I know things about you. You lost your virginity with your brother's math tutor. You were sixteen, he was twenty-three. You seduced him in the music room when your parents took your brother to soccer."

"I tried to seduce him, he said no," I murmured. In my mind, a split-screen opened up. On one half, set in Brian's imaginary alternate universe, I was sixteen again, all skinny limbs and a big mouth freshly released from braces. I was passionately kissing that math tutor. I could still see how hot he was: burly and dark-haired with clean-cut features that belonged on a movie actor, not on a math nerd. Then I unbuttoned his shirt, and I could almost . . . almost . . . feel the juicy triumph of the moment.

On the other half of the screen of my mind, in the real world as I knew it, I remembered running my hands along the tutor's shoulders. He turned away, told me I was too young and innocent, and to stop it because I didn't know what I was doing. I had never felt so vulnerable.

Not long after that, David had a party. His parents were out of town, and I finagled to get him alone in a closet and have my way with him. After that, we'd been together more or less forever. . . . Until three years ago.

"There was no rejection in my world, Lolita," Brian said. He was peering closely into my face, must have seen the emotions chasing themselves across it.

I shook my head and grinned. "My mom was sick upstairs in bed. I was so humiliated. But no one knows about that, not even Ofee!"

Brian raised my hand to his lips and kissed my palm. "You love red wine, but you're allergic to it. You sometimes get a histamine reaction. Here." He released my hand and gave me a folded photograph.

I was suspicious but I opened it. There I was, smiling back at me, radiant in a big white wedding dress with a gossamer veil floating around me like a white aura. On either side of me stood Ofee and Brian, both in tuxedoes.

"It's photoshopped," I stated, though a shiver went along my spine. "Ofee would never wear a tuxedo, not in any universe."

"Happiest day of my life!" Brian said.

"Do you need medication? This is a really elaborate stalker gig." I held out the photo for him to take.

Brian secreted it back on his person. His eyes were effervescent when they returned to me. "Let's go back to your apartment. One of your drawings showed people having sex."

"None of my drawings shows people having sex! And neither are we. From now on, we're strictly platonic."

But it wasn't a vow I could keep when we got back to my apartment. Brian kissed me in that inscrutably irresistible way that highjacked my good sense, and I blamed my lack of willpower on the red wine and my histamine reaction.

Too bad I didn't get a histamine reaction in this world.

17 Nine of spades

The next morning, I left a note for Brian next to him on the bed where he was still sleeping soundly. "Thanks for everything, you're amazing, please leave," read the note. "PS, I saved the last yogurt in the fridge for your breakfast. Please put my skull on the kitchen table."

I was in my office helping Mr. Jenkins figure out his amplifier telephone when cacophony erupted in the church. I had a sinking feeling, and when I peeked out into the church, sure enough, there in the nave was Brian performing magic for a crowd. He was clumsy and obvious, narrating his inept trickery with jolly, oblivious patter. It made me groan. I slammed my office door shut.

"EH?" shouted Mr. Jenkins.

"Nothing, nothing, Mr. Jenkins," I said, waving him to silence. I took a moment to think deeply. What to do, what to do?

Then I grabbed my cell phone. It was still working, though for how much longer, I didn't know. My mobile bill was getting a little stale. I peered out through a crack in the door and waited for my best friend to answer his cell phone, half a world away.

"Tessy, sweetheart, is that you?" Ofee drawled.

"Ofee, I miss you!" I cried.

"I miss you too, Tessy, but I only have a moment. I'm actually in Scorpio pose right now. Demonstrating for my students."

I had a flash of Ofee, unibrow and all, twisting himself into a pretzel while talking on the phone to me. In the background, beautiful Thai people served fruit and drinks to impressed onlookers.

"Okay, sweetie. Don't you still do privates with the dean's wife at Columbia? Have you heard of a guy named Brian Tennyson?"

"Brian who? Oh, wait, yeah. The physicist. He's an author, too," Ofee said. His voice changed timbre, and I could tell he was transitioning to a different pose.

"What pose?" I asked. "You mean he's a real professor?"

"Flying crow," Ofee said. He raised his voice, speaking to someone near him. "That's great, Martin, what do you call that, Sleeping Warrior with piña colada? Just breathe." His voice returned to a softer tone. “Tessy, I heard some gossip. He went crazy. Break with reality. Institutionalized. Big scandal.”

That makes sense. I opened my office door wider to see what was going on.

Brian was trying to summon a quarter from elderly Mrs. Simon’s ear while doing a card trick for a choir singer. He yanked the old lady’s wig, pulling it askew.

I yelped. “Gotta go, love you!” I threw down my cell phone and darted toward Brian.

“Here, Blue Eyes, pick a card.” Brain fanned out a deck of cards and held it toward the choir singer, who obliged.

“Help, I can’t see through my hair,” quavered Mrs. Simon.

The choir singer replaced the card in the deck.

Brian grasped Mrs. Simon’s wig and righted it. He dropped half the deck, saved the other half, and triumphantly held up a single card. “Shazam, the nine of spades!”

“I drew the three of diamonds,” said the blue-eyed choir singer.

“I’m sure it was the nine of spades,” Brian insisted.

“Three of—”

“Brian, time for lunch,” I said, reaching through the group. “Let’s go.”

"Tessa, I missed you this morning. That wine last night really zonked me out." He nuzzled and then kissed me.

I tried to push him off me and lead him away, but he turned back to the choir singer and resumed arguing good-naturedly.

Naturally, Reverend Pincek chose that moment to bustle up and join us. "Tessa, I didn't know you had a boyfriend."

"He's not my boyfriend."

"Well, he seems very nice," the rev said. "Maybe he could entertain the kids at our Saturday open house. Will he work for free?"

"He's only in town for a few days," I said, hurriedly, to dispel such a disastrous notion.

But Brian suddenly tuned in. "I'm here until Sunday afternoon. I love kids. I wanted some of my own." He smiled and shook the rev's hand. "Dr. Brian Tennyson, nice to meet you."

Reverend Pincek clapped him on the shoulder with approval. "Henry Ward Beecher said, 'Children are the hands by which we take hold of heaven.' You're a fine young man, Dr. Tennyson, I'm sure you'll have fine sons and daughters yet."

The blue-eyed choir singer drew Brian back into the debate, and the rev turned to me. In as quiet a voice as he could manage, which was not quiet at all, the rev asked, "Did you hear that, Tessa? He's nice, and he's a doctor."

"Not that kind of doctor," I started.

Joan, the secretary, charged up with a sheaf of papers, saving me from an explanation that could only cast serious aspersions on my own character. What the hell was I doing sleeping with a crazy man?

What the hell was I doing with my life?

The one question I didn't ask myself, which I probably should have, was what the hell was I doing with the Bucknell skull?

"Come on, Brian, let's go." I took hold of his arm firmly and pulled him away. "You brought it, right? I have to meet Guy."

Brian opened his mouth to say something, but the rev cut us off at the door.

"Tessa, I have to ask you to take some time off. We found a plumbing leak. Our funds–"

I shook my head. "I can't duck out, Rev. People depend on me. Pay when you can."

"We're pretty broke right now," the rev rumbled. "I hate to take advantage. You know we want to pay you."

"A donation will come through soon," I promised.

"I don't think so," Brian said, with a rueful smile.

"I do," I said and tread heavily on his foot.

“We’re certainly praying for one,” said Reverend Pincek.

“While we wait for the answer to our prayers, tell me, Rev, are you charging for the senior dance?” Brian asked. He draped his arm around me with casual familiarity, as if we’d been married for ten years. “You know, to raise money.”

The rev and I exchanged a look. I said, “Most people who come to eldercare are on fixed incomes. They live on social security.”

The rev scratched his chin. “It’s a nice idea, Brian, but we don’t want to add to their financial burdens. The new health care laws have strained the tight budgets of the elderly to the breaking point.”

“Some of them are even forgoing medications because of the new financial burdens,” I added. “The government passed a law and didn’t bother to think about how real people would be able foot the bill.” Some of the money I made at the church had been spent on Mr. James’ costly medicine. “It was the triumph of philosophy over humanity,” I said. “Of course, the health insurance companies are just getting richer than ever.”

“Not another one of your rants,” Brian said firmly, holding up his hand. He thought for a moment. “Charge non-elderly people. Make it an everyone dance, a family dance. Get the teens in here. Little kids. Charge anyone under sixty-five. You might not get a lot of people, but hey, I'd take my granny to a dance for an hour to make her happy. And if there's food involved . . . "

I have to admit, the rev and I were dumbfounded. Neither of us had ever considered such a radical idea. I said slowly, "We'd have to spread the word fast."

"There must be an email list for the congregation," Brian said.

"We can put it up on our website," the rev sang.

"We can put up a sign on the door," I enthused. I could visualize it, and I'd get to try out some of that new titanium white . . . .

"The Bible study group meets Wednesday nights," Reverend Pincek said.

"Tonight!" I exclaimed. "They're a gossipy bunch."

"This could work," the rev said. "Everyone's welcome, kids under ten are free. That might bring in some of the young families, too."

"Kids under five are free," Brian said. "And park some big jars around for contributions."

"I'll get volunteers right on it," the rev said, with excitement. He galloped off.

Brian squeezed me in one of his bear hugs.

I pushed him away. As I moved forward, my foot wobbled. Not now! The heel of my shoe was broken. "Right when I have to meet Guy."

"It's a sign," Brian leered at me playfully, "for us to go home and cuddle. Then go see Frances."

I took off my shoe and glared at the offending heel. "What part of 'no' do you not understand, the 'N' or the 'O'?"

"You know you want to," Brian said. "You have to give back the skull. Do it now. Frances is a good guy, he'll understand that you only meant to help the rev."

But I had a better idea, and I dug in my bag for a role of duct tape which I brandished victoriously. "I can fix my shoe. I can do anything with duct tape!"

"Oh, brother." Brian sighed. "I'll go home and make lunch. Do you have any money for me to buy food, or am I using that tub of laundry quarters I found in your linen closet?"

"You're coming with me, mister," I said. "I'm not letting you out of my sight until I have the skull. I think you have it on you."

18 Modern art

The Rothschild Gallery was even more pretentious than the Frances Gates Gallery. Rooms were dimly lit, swathes of fabric hung down, and flatscreen TVs shared wall space with exceptionally atrocious abstract art.

Naturally, there was a rave review from *The New York Times* prominently placed in every room.

"This is the ugliness of ugliness. This crap makes me want to kill myself," I muttered.

"Tessa, sweetheart, life is always right. Don't even joke that way," Brian said.

We moved from room to room. I was supposed to meet Guy here, but I didn't see him among the black-clad hipsters. I spied a partly open door in back. "Let's check this one," I said.

We entered a large empty room that wasn't quite as dark as the rest of the gallery. There wasn't anything in the room except some red lights high in the corners, glowing like red demon eyes. I must have been grimacing to myself because Brian stroked my cheek and shoulder.

"The stuff looks like a four-year-old crayoned it, but why do you care so much? Why let it trigger you?"

"Art can be so much more," I murmured. I leaned into Brian's warm, solid chest. It had been so long since a man had held me with love and support. Truth be told, my ex had never been good at that. He hadn't held me much physically, other than our sporadic conjugal connections. He hadn't held me emotionally at all.

"What, exactly, can art be for you?" Brian asked. He nuzzled me and drew me closer in to his body, as if he craved me.

This was it, the central, ineluctable question of my life: what can art be for me? I had never framed it this way, but hearing Brian articulate it opened up something.

Could art be my livelihood? It was certainly my passion. But could it sustain me?

And what did it mean to me, apart from the material aspects?

I bilocated into the Louvre, so that I stood in front of the sweeping Daru Staircase. I was a young girl looking up to the gorgeous rippling *Winged Victory*. "My eighth grade French class went to Paris, to the Louvre. I walked up the stairs to the *Winged Victory*, and I was smitten! It's so beautiful and full of life, timeless and eternal. Looking at it, all the mundane stuff of life fell away. All the petty misery. I was healed, I was exalted. I was transformed. That's what real art does!"

"Fair enough, this stuff isn't art," Brian observed. His words pulled me back to the Rothschild Modern and the schlocky degraded stuff that passed for art at even the most exclusive galleries. Brian waved toward the door. "It's entertainment. So what?"

"So these commodities corrupt art as a field," I cried, willing him to understand.

"Why not take a stand against it by making beautiful art? Not by stealing. But by showing your own art. Your paintings are beautiful—people will buy them."

I gulped and covered my face with my hands. "I may have made some stupid choices in the past. Bad choices."

"Choices that keep you from painting?"

"It's complicated."

"Sweetheart, you can't hold on to the past that way. Whatever you've done, own it, apologize, make amends if you can, and then move on." He nestled me closer in to the crook of his neck and shoulder and kissed my forehead.

"My reputation . . . "

"Fuck your reputation," Brian said, but tenderly. "You're young and alive. As long as you're breathing, you have a chance. To make things right, to make a fresh start. It's a gift."

"You don't understand," I whispered.

Brian kissed me more deeply on my mouth. "Want to explain?"

"No," I said, but Brian was still kissing me, and the gallery faded away, and I started to respond. What luscious magic hold over me did this man have to elicit such arousal?

He picked up my hand and kissed my palm.

"Mm, you know I can't resist that," I moaned. Everything in me softened and opened. I lost myself in the breathlessness of the moment with him, and it didn't matter that we were in a gallery. We could have been anywhere in the world, a crowded bazaar, or Grand Central Station, or alone in this quiet room. I simply wanted him.

"Tessa, you're a sweet, caring, beautiful woman and a gifted artist. In my world and here. Stop beating up on yourself. You're alive, and you'll figure it all out. It will work out." He kissed my neck and clavicles.

I groaned, my hips churning against him. Then I leapt up into his arms, wrapping my legs around him. I didn't know what I was doing, but lately, I never did. It didn't seem to matter because I was so desperate to change my life.

I still didn't realize that I would have to change myself first.

Brian pushed me up against the wall next to the door. I vaguely saw his hand close and lock the door. Then someone's shirt fluttered out into the air.

19 Performance art and real talent

We finally emerged from the empty room, and I made sure to straighten my skirt. My shirt was buttoned incorrectly, so I hurriedly redid it.

Gallery patrons were clustered around the flatscreens. A woman with kohl-smeared raccoon eyes and a beehive hairdo spied us. She began to clap. The sound drew everyone else's attention, and they first stared and then clapped as well. A few people called, "Bravo! Bravo!"

"What the hell?" I wondered.

A distinguished looking older man pushed through the crowd. There was no mistaking his tall form and the distinct, craggy features of his distinct, craggy face. He loved himself with the steamy, torrid self-congratulation of a thousand suns, something that had once impressed me.

Now it made me want to vomit.

"Well done, Tess, good to see you. Nice work in there," he said, in a faux British accent that, I regret to say, had also once impressed me.

Had I been brain damaged back then?

"Cliff Bucknell," I said slowly.

Cliff took my tone as the adulation he usually received and he preened. "So now you're into performance art. Give up on those cheesy landscapes? There's just no point to them. Beauty is so banal. Post-modernism is all about the anti-aesthetic. That's the cutting edge. What's really evocative isn't evocative at all."

Once upon a time, this kind of posturing had enthralled me. Now, and maybe it had something to do with how warm and real Crazy Brian was, it seemed silly.

I asked, "What are you doing here?"

Brian, his arm looped around my waist, interjected, "Why do I get the feeling that we were the stars of some show?"

A slithery man dressed all in black stepped forward. "Great performance! An intense expression of scatological yearning."

"That wasn't scatological," Brian started. He did a double take. "What exactly did you see?"

"Everything," said the slithery man. "I'm opening an installation at the MOMA entitled ‘Altogether Human Beings,’ and I’d love to have you perform your piece there. It’s been recorded here, but I prefer performance art to be live.”

“Recorded?” I reeled backward. “Cliff, you saw . . . ?”

“Even in lovemaking, you’re, oh, idealistic and enthusiastic, but hackneyed. But then, that isn’t your real talent, is it?” Cliff laughed shortly, his eyes gleaming.

Brian growled, literally, growled. He stepped up to Cliff and pushed him, hard. “Watch how you talk to her, buddy. And what are you talking about, ‘real talent’?”

Cliff puffed out his chest but he receded a few steps. “She knows. Quite a useful gift for the shadow arts, even if she’ll never be a real artist. She made a reputation for herself.”

I fled.

Brian chased me.

As we passed the front door, Guy, smoking a cigarette, stepped in my way. “The contribution of shadows is to make the light shine out all the more, and even that which can be considered ugly in itself appears beautiful within the framework of the general order. It is this order as a whole that is beautiful, but from this standpoint even monstrosity is redeemed—"

"Not now!" I cried, half heartbroken, half outraged.

"Call me, if you value your thumbs," Guy said.

20 Apple of my eye

Fourteenth Street teemed with pedestrians and a profusion of shops. I stormed along it with my shirt and jacket buttoned askew, my taped-on heel wobbling.

As if I hadn't bungled my past enough, now I was headlining in art porn. Could I sink any lower? This was all Brian's fault. "You had no right to seduce me," I spat at him.

"You wrapped your legs around me, what was I gonna say, 'No thanks'?"

"Yes, if you were a gentleman." I was really steaming.

Brian laughed. "Right. Who was that pretentious old guy with the fake accent, and what was he talking about, 'shadow arts'?"

"That's Cliff Bucknell. He's the darling of the art world, the next Warhol."

"He's the guy who made the skull?" Brian asked.

"He's the guy whose name is on the skull. I haven't seen him in three years. How does he know I haven't been painting?" Was I so transparently, humiliatingly obvious?

"You're painting now," Brian pointed out. "You painted that beautiful landscape over the eviction notice. And all those canvases in your living room and hall closet."

"Those are from three years ago. I haven't painted since then, until this week."

"My Tessa would never stop playing the cello because of a little rejection," Brian said, in a puzzled tone. "What happened to you? Tessa, sometimes, to move forward in life, you have to take risks—"

"Risks, I'll show you risks," I said. I burst into a sprint. My taped-on heel cracked off. Duct tape had its limitations, as we all do. I kicked my shoe into the street, where it was run over by a taxi and flattened pancake-style. Hobbling with one bare foot, I ran into the Apple store.

The store was, as always, completely thronged with people of all ages and sizes and nationalities. If I had held still, which I did not, I would have heard twenty different languages being spoken.

"Tessa, your foot, take my shoe," said Brian, panting.

I shouldered a punk teenager off the latest sleek, sexy iMac. My fingers tapped madly on the keyboard. "Google Brian Tennyson," I muttered.

"No, this isn't a good idea, don't," said Brian, with a tone of alarm. He grabbed my arm.

"What are you afraid of finding out?" I shook him off. "Brian Tennyson, all over the web, lookee here. I know about you, Brian," I said, triumphantly. "You're a professor who had a psychotic break from reality and had to be hospitalized."

"I am not!" Brian said, indignantly. "That never happened, not in any universe."

"Home page at Columbia? Maybe it mentions the institutionalization," I mused.

Brian couldn't help himself, he crowded in next to me and peered over my shoulder. A page lauding Dr. Brian Tennyson filled the screen, showcasing his many honors and distinctions. He was a slicker, more polished version than the other-worldly Brian who had followed me around and tumbled into my bed. He really was down on his luck. I had a flash of sympathy for him.

"I heard you were an author, but wow, three books. What a shame such a promising young professor had to be put in an asylum."

"Books?" Brian asked, pushing me aside.

A spiffy Apple salesman approached us. "Hey, folks, my name is Jordan. Check out how blazing fast the new iMac is."

"This one is a best seller," I pointed around Brian's torso at the screen. "It was for the general public."

"*How the Enterprise Can Beam Us Up*! I loved it. This is you? Let me get Chad, he's a Trekkie, and he totally gets off on your book." Jordan tripped off, wriggling with excitement like a puppy.

"I haven't published any books in my world," Brian muttered, softly. His eyes clouded over.

"No books in dreamworld? You aren't taking risks in hallucination land, Oh Beautiful Mind?" I asked tartly.

"Thank you, but it's not about risks for me, it's about priorities. Who cares about papers and books and awards? My marriage matters to me. I spent my time with you, not locked away in an office, and I'm so glad I did!" Brian looked ready to burst.

Jordan and another eager-beaver genius had joined us. "Dr. Tennyson, this is Chad."

"Dude, you're a rock star!" Chad enthused, pumping Brian's hand with even more enthusiasm than Brian usually displayed. "The way you explain the wave function of the universe is awesome. Are you writing a new book?"

"He's too busy living out his hallucinations," I started.

Brian swung around on me. "For Pete's sake, Tessa. You're just mad because everyone watched us on the TVs in that stupid art gallery making love."

Yes, I was mad, damn it. Rightfully so. "Don't you realize, Rothschild will run that pornographic video of us on an endless loop until something stupider and kinkier comes along!"

Jordan asked, "What's the name of the gallery?"

"That was pretty kinky," Brian said, scratching at his beard stubble. "What did we do, five different positions? I felt inspired, and you were oh, so willing."

"What kind of crack is that?" I demanded.

"Is that Rothschild Modern or Rothschild Masters?" murmured Jordan, fingers flying over the keyboard.

Brian wasn't done harassing me. He said, "It wasn't stupid, it was enthusiastic. You had a good time. Good thing, because you needed one."

What the hell? "What's that supposed to mean?" I demanded, frost chilling my words, and, I hoped, withering him into his place.

"That I built my many worlds device and arrived here not a moment too soon," Brian responded in a tone that matched mine. "You were so horny, you squeaked when you walked. If I'd arrived any later, you'd have been humping trees."

I was getting ready to let Brian have it when Chad jostled me out of the way.

"Many worlds device?" interrupted Chad. "Is that what I think it is, Dr. Tennyson? Wow, if you invented that, you're like Da Vinci, a real polymath superbrain!"

"Thank you," Brian said. "I don't mean to sound immodest, but I accept your praise. It is a great achievement."

"Don't you dare mention one of the great Renaissance masters in the same breath as this lunatic," I said hotly, immersing myself in the incomparable *Virgin of the Rocks* and its glorious sfumato. "Da Vinci was a one-of-a-kind master. His use of perspective and psychological portraiture—"

"Dr. T's book was genius," gushed Chad. "I loved the story about Einstein writing to his friend for help on the math for relativity."

Brian posed and affected a German accent. "Grossman, you must help me or I'll go crazy!"

"Erp," squeaked Jordan. His eyebrows climbed up over his hairline and it sent an inaudible signal for other Apple geniuses to gather around him, watching what he found online.

"Then Grossman accidentally came across the

math. Einstein was stuck until someone else stumbled on it. It's like these little chance happenings that affect everything," said Chad in a tone of awe. "Makes you wonder, what would have happened if Grossman hadn't found the math?"

Customers around the store buzzed as they clustered around computer screens, from which spilled out heavy breathing and kissing noises. I stepped in toward Jordan, tried to wend myself through the geniuses gathered around him so I could see the screen better. That couldn't possibly be the video of Brian and me, posted on the Internet already, could it?

"I love metric tensors," Brian said. "I used them in my invention to prove macroscopic decoherence."

"So there'll be another book?" asked Chad.

"Maybe," Brian said, smiling. "I've discovered that it's possible to build a device to traverse parallel worlds, using magnetic portals that link the sun to the earth. Would be a great book."

"Magnetic portals?" chirped Chad. But then he glanced at the screen and did a double take. I tried to push him aside but he was rooted to his spot.

"Shut it down!" bellowed a senior-management-looking type who ran out from the back and waved his arms furiously. That's when I caught a brief glimpse of naked, intertwined limbs to go with the soft, luscious moaning that emanated from every screen in the store. I felt a lightning strike of anxiety.

Brian didn't pick up on anything, he was so caught up in his imaginary science. "Flux transfer events. Because of the flowing through of tons of high-energy particles, they generate the conditions for many worlds travel."

"Shut it down!" hollered the manager again.

I had had enough for the twentieth time in the last two days. Had it only been two days? It felt like a lifetime. "Would you please let go of your delusions," I hissed. "Look around you. Do you know what they're watching? I think it's us. I didn't need you to show up in my life and stalk me and seduce me."

"Oh, yeah, you did," said Brian. "You're the one who's lost in a fantasy world of taking care of old people and punishing yourself for your past and living in the tomb of your failed marriage."

"My marriage didn't fail, I failed," I said. The manager of the Apple store was running from one Mac to the next and pounding on the keyboards.

Brian shook his head. "That's so neurotic. You have to cut that loose. David was never meant for you. He's too rigid. You're a kooky piece of work who needs a lot of holding. I could do that."

"Not everything revolves around you. Or sex," I

said. "I've got plenty of fulfilling relationships. I'm going to visit Mrs. Leibowitz."

"That's not a relationship," Brian said. "That's you taking care of a dying old lady."

The video had reached a climax. My own ecstatic cries filled the Apple store. It was like one of those nightmares where you're naked in public, only it was real. I was horrified into stillness like a pillar of salt.

The Apple store manager sagged back against the display table and covered his face with his hands.

"Dr. T, wow," said Chad. "You are a true genius!"

"You gave the lady a good time," said Jordan with admiration. He led the other geniuses in applauding Brian. Everyone joined in except some children whose eyes were shielded by their mothers. The store reverberated with thunderous acclaim.

Brian held up his arms in the victory sign and bowed.

"How dare you!" I could feel myself flushing scarlet.

"I dare," said Brian. "I take risks."

There was no escaping it, I was going to have to live with the embarrassment. Hadn't I become an expert at intimacy with my own shame? I flounced towards the door while holding my head high. My uneven limping spoiled my dramatic exit until I realized I didn't have to wear only one shoe. Turning around, I took it off and flung it at Brian, who ducked.

"Dude, good thing you already got some," Jordan said. "Because I don't think you're getting any more."

"I've never actually had my own woman, so I don't understand them," Chad added. "But I'm pretty sure that when they throw a shoe at you, it's not good."

Brian was staring at me with a look that was almost baleful. "No one, not physicists, not even Einstein, not the most brilliant genius of all physicists who comes up with the grand unified theory of everything in one simple equation, understands women!"

Didn't he get it? "I lost everything because of the risks I've taken," I said. I left the store.

I'd had enough insult with my injury.

21 Cavemen and peeky-toe stilettos

I knelt by Mrs. Leibowitz's closet and pulled out a pair of outrageously fluffy, sequined turquoise slippers. Old-fashioned silk dresses swirled around my head, muffling my voice.

"You don't mind me borrowing these?" I yelled to be heard through the fabric.

"You don't have to shout, dear, my hearing still works," said Mrs. L. "I only wish my feet were your size, and you could have some real shoes."

"These are perfect," I assured her. "No heels for me to break."

"Tessa, there's only one antidote to breaking heels."

I climbed out of the closet and perched expectantly in the chair beside Mrs. L's bed. I recognized that arch tone, and I knew from our long association that she would come out with something funny and unexpected. "Okay, I'll bite. What's that, Mrs. L?"

"Four-inch high, peeky-toe, patent leather, fuck-me-now stilettos!" Mrs. Leibowitz grinned.

"Mrs. Leibowitz!" I remonstrated, laughing.

"Nothing makes a round ass look more enticing. The stilettos give you a wiggle, and men can't resist that. Brian would love it." She cut her eyes at me.

I sighed. "Brian is psychotic."

"He's eccentric. Scientists are like that."

"Brian is way further along the cuckoo scale than eccentric." I scowled.

Mrs. L shook her head. "My generation wasn't so hung up about sex. In fact, we invented kinky sex."

"Cavemen did that," I demurred, "which explains why men are all so fixated on sex. Even scientists. They're all really cavemen."

"Oh no, you don't understand, it was my generation that really explored kink," Mrs. L insisted. "We were desperate to get away from the war. You wouldn't believe the naughty things Bernie and I did."

I laughed helplessly, but I didn't inquire. I didn't want to know. "Why don't I take you outside? It's another nice day."

"I don't think so," she said, and melted into her pillows. "Could you push the bureau so it's flush with the end of the bed? I like looking at the photos."

I got up and strained to push the heavy mahogany bureau. "Are you tired again today, Mrs. L? Are you taking your meds?"

"Just a small shift to change the perspective," she murmured. "I don't feel like going out or seeing anyone. Just you, Tessa, you're so bright and dear. Suddenly you're very spirited, too. But I'm not. I'm winding down like an old watch. I want to do that in peace."

My heart clutched in on itself. "A full care facility—"

"I'm staying here," she said firmly. "Bernie and I lived here in this apartment for fifty years. It's full of us, of our life together. Keeps me from being lonely."

I stood by her bed and picked up her hand and stroked it. "Mrs. L, you can't take care of yourself. What would have happened to you yesterday if I hadn't come along when I did? You could have been sitting out there all night."

"I get myself food when I'm hungry, and I have clean clothes."

"You need more care than that," I said, but gently because she was dear to me and I didn't want to upset her.

"No, I don't. I don't want to have a lot of tubes running into my arms and medicines pumped into me. I don't want to lie in some strange bed at the mercy of strangers. What an inhumane way to die!"

"You could have a lot of time left, and the quality of that time—"

"Is up to me," she stated. She gave me a solemn look. "The quality of anyone's life is always up to them. Everyone chooses how they feel in any set of circumstances. I always feel my love for Bernie and our children. Now I'm unraveling, and I don't mind. After ninety years, that's what happens. That's what's supposed to happen. Oh, there's a gift for you. On the bureau."

I wanted to argue with her that she should let herself live, that half a life was still precious. One look at her set face told me it was pointless. Wonderful, she was; easy, not so much. I found a rectangular brown-paper package on the bureau. "What's this?"

"Wait to open it until this weekend," Mrs. L said. "Saturday. Open it after Saturday."

"You didn't have to do this, Mrs. Leibowitz."

"I know. I wanted to," she said in a soft, slow voice. "Doing what you want is the prerogative of the dying. Should be the prerogative of the living, too, but it doesn't always work out that way."

"I don't want you to die!"

22 Where the past meets the future

Brian stood outside my building. Next to him were a stack of my canvases and two suitcases. He was holding my laptop computer under one arm and my drawing pads under the other.

I sprinted toward him, turquoise slippers slapping the sidewalk. "Brian, what's going on?" I cried.

"José changed your locks. Luckily, he let me in to get your stuff. He's a good guy."

"The board locked me out?"

"They want you to make a substantial payment toward what you owe. They're actually trying to avoid court." Brian shrugged.

"This isn't legal, it can't be," I said.

"We're here now, what do we do?"

"Damn it! How much do they want?"

"Twelve thousand dollars and a payment schedule."

"Okay, okay." I ran my hands through my hair, thinking fast. "Give me the skull. I'll call Guy right now. He probably already has a buyer in mind, that's why he's so intense about the skull. We can do it quick."

"That Guy, he is one strange dude. I don't like him."

"Me neither," I admitted, shuddering. "Let's get him off my back."

Brian scratched his chin. "About that. I put the skull in your cupboard where the wine was."

I stared at Brian with growing, sinking comprehension. I plopped down, sitting on the suitcase. "It's still in my apartment."

"Yes."

"You don't have the skull with you."

"No. And we have a bigger problem. Frances gave me one day to get you to give back the skull. Then he's calling the police." Brian seated himself next to me.

"Better the police than Guy," I said, and shivered.

"You need a strategy so you don't have to face either one," Brian said quietly.

"A strategy? I need another life!"

"You have one. Billions even," Brian said, in a voice that was both bitter and nostalgic.

"I mean here and now in the real world, Professor." I felt bitter myself. All my eggs were hatching, and buzzards with poison talons were emerging.

"What about making a head? Say it's yours and give it to Guy to sell. As your copy of Bucknell's copy of Hirst's thing. That would pass as clever in the art market."

That's when I lost it. After everything. I dropped my head into my hands and wept.

Brian exclaimed and stroked my hair.

"It is my skull. I made it." I sobbed so deeply the words barely made it out.

"I don't understand."

"Cliff mentioned the shadow arts . . . ."

"He meant forgery?" Brian asked with an indrawn breath.

I nodded. Then, because I couldn't help it, couldn't keep the doors to my memory banged shut as firmly as I'd been able to until this very moment, I remembered three years ago.

The scene was Cliff Bucknell's studio in the Catskills. I was working on the skull, gluing on sequins. It was the last piece I was making for him, the final one, after other projects I'd finished for him or spoon fed to him. I talked to Cliff while I worked, hoping to rouse him.

Cliff was lying in bed curled up in a fetal position. He'd succumbed to heroin, a steady spiral down into depression, inertia, and then paralysis after his romance with pot and cocaine. He'd stopped working and had failed to honor several contracts with galleries and private patrons; he was in danger of being sued and ignominiously cast out by the art world that had hitherto idolized him.

Then came I, the good and empathic student, to the rescue.

The memory faded with its usual sting. I picked up my head to look Brian in the eyes. It felt good to come clean. "Cliff was clinically depressed and hooked on drugs. I was his student and I wanted to help him—"

"Yeah, and I know how you help in this world. At your own expense," Brian said angrily.

I shrugged and didn't look away. "He had contractual obligations with dealers, galleries, and with Guy. So I started a cottage industry of making his pieces for him. I also suggested work for him and modeled for him. Remember the nudes at Frances's gallery? That was me."

Brian stiffened. "You posed naked for him? Were you sleeping with him?"

Another painful memory: I stood naked in front

of Cliff, who stood at an easel in a silk robe. He was a wreck, barely functional, this once celebrated figure in the art world, and disintegrating in front of my eyes. He couldn't even keep up his phony accent but sounded like the Bronx boy he'd been.

Then David walked in—I still hadn't figured out why my husband came to Cliff's studio that day—and he made the obvious assumption. He didn't say a word. He gave me a look of contempt, turned on his heel, and swept out in disgust.

Didn't he owe me a few questions after our years together?

Didn't I owe it to us to point that out to him? Or was I just glad to get the demise of my marriage over with?

I took a deep breath. "I didn't sleep with Cliff, but everyone thought I did, especially David."

"Saint David, your first choice," Brian spat.

"Brian, my ex was no saint," I said and then resumed the pitiful tale. "One of the dealers realized that Cliff's work wasn't actually Cliff's work. He told galleries that Cliff was being taken advantage of because he was ill. It spread like lightening that Cliff's assistant, me, was passing off her work as Cliff's and pocketing the proceeds. I never got a penny, but I was instantly the Osama Bin Laden of the art world—a hated pariah. No one blamed Cliff because he's, well, Cliff. They blamed me. David was disgusted and wouldn't let me explain." And maybe I didn't want to, I realized.

Brian sprang up and paced in circles around me and the suitcases. "I can't believe this. Forgery, cheating. Who are you?"

"Your wife in another life," I said, bitterly. "I can tell you what I'm not: a thief. The skull belongs to me, Brian. It was never supposed to be sold. Cliff promised to give it to me. He even signed a letter authenticating it as mine and belonging to me. I don't know how that skull ended up in Frances Gates's gallery, but I have legal claim to it. It's mine. Gates didn't do his homework on the piece's provenance. The letter's in a drawer in my bedroom. I'm surprised you didn't find it when you went through my stuff."

"I got waylaid by your thongs," Brian quipped. His gaze on me softened. "I knew you weren't a thief." He knelt in front of me. "You know why I came here?"

"God, I've asked myself that question," I said. I gave him a tearful lopsided smile, which was all I had in me. "You escaped the institution and found me somehow on the Internet?"

"You still don't believe that I am who I say I am? Even after sleeping with me? Fine. I came here because you're alive."

"So what?"

"So in my world, you aren't." Brian said. He closed his eyes, and in the air floating around him like an aura, I could almost, *almost*, tangibly see Tessa, me, gaunt, lying in bed and hooked to an IV. Brian crawled into the hospital bed and wrapped his arms around me, *her*, the other me. Her eyes closed and the image of her face rolled away.

"Melanoma. From that mole on your breast, so they treated you for breast cancer. When they discovered the mistake, it was too late. Your death almost killed me. I became obsessed with seeing you again. That's why I built the decoherence device. I'd been noodling around with the many worlds theory for years. But when you were gone . . .

"It was never about my career or scientific advancement or the Nobel Prize or any of that nonsense. It was about you. The woman I love. My everything.

"So don't complain about the mistakes you made in the past, because you still have a future." He plopped down next to me on the suitcase. Anguished, he combed his fingers through his hair so it stood straight up.

Cars and pedestrians passed. Golden light slanted down from the sun. I looked up at the ribbon of blue sky, the leafy green branches of trees, and the pale fingernail moon in the sky. To the west, over the Hudson River that I couldn't see but could imagine so well, clouds made contrails over the indigo water. I had a flash of a landscape painting. It was a cityscape, and on the sidewalk were two small, distinct figures full of loss, somehow mysteriously connected.

I rose. "I have the keys to Ofee's place. We'll go there while I figure out what to do."

Brian was staring at my feet. "Great slippers."

23 Downward facing dog solves all the problems of life

Ofee's walls were covered with posters of Ganesh, lotus flowers, and seated meditators with colorful chakras. One of my landscapes—a rather nice rendering of the Shawangunk Ridge in New Paltz in the fall, when the leaves had burst into colors of flame—hung beside Alex Grey's visionary anatomical bodies. Brian and I dragged in the suitcases and canvases.

"We have a place to stay. But I'm so upset I can't think of what to do. I have to make a plan," I said, wringing my hands.

Brian walked around, examining Ofee's décor. "Clearly Ofee is a drug dealer in this world. As a rule, I don't believe in illegal substances, but this is an emergency. We'll find his stash and see what he has that will make you feel better."

I couldn't help smiling reluctantly. "Ofee's not a

drug dealer. He's a yoga teacher. Well known, with a cult following."

Brian cracked up. "Ofee teaches yoga!"

"He claims that downward facing dog solves all the problems of life." I kicked off the fluffy turquoise slippers and demonstrated the pose.

Brian walked around behind me and stared appreciatively at my ass.

I looked up at him from between my legs and saw some of his native ebullience return.

Brian placed his hands lightly on my hips. "Ofee's on to something, absotively, posilutely."

"Nope. I'm still broke, divorced, homeless, and a failed painter with a shady past. Now there's a porno art video of me on the Internet." I collapsed onto my back. "Could things get worse?"

"Dead is worse," Brian said, his voice unsteady. He waited a beat, then spoke normally. "Anyway, you look really hot in the video. More importantly, so do I. That's not so easy for a physicist." He sat down beside me on the floor.

"So, I'm still alive and kicking. What's Ofee do in your hypothetical world?"

"He's a tax lawyer."

Now it was my turn to gargle with disbelieving laughter. "No way, there's no possible world where Ofee is a lawyer!"

"You don't believe in alternate worlds. You think I'm a kook."

"True. Sorry."

Brian flicked hair out of my eyes. He kissed the bridge of my nose. "I guess I'll just have to prove it to you. You think Ofee has a hat, or a wig, or something in this place so I can disguise myself?"

"We can probably find something," I murmured. "Why?"

"Because I'm taking you to a public lecture I saw advertised online today, when we were at the Apple store."

24 Level IV universes

Brian wore a blonde starlet wig we found in one of Ofee's closets. I wondered why Ofee owned it because he'd never mentioned such a thing to me. Did he have a hidden life as a transvestite that I didn't know about? Who even needed parallel worlds, when we could live out many lives in this one? There are so many secrets people keep from one another, even best friends.

But I suppose those aren't as precarious as the secrets we keep from ourselves.

"This is a good look for me," Brian said, stroking the long, shiny locks of hair. We emerged from the subway stop at 116th Street on the Upper West Side. I knew where we were, of course: Columbia University, where I'd spent four years as an art major.

What were we doing here now? I had not a clue. Brian had been unusually circumspect, though chipper. I glanced at him. "It's the mirror shades that make the look."

"I know, right?" he sang, and chortled.

If he hugged me right now, I'd slug him. I still hadn't forgiven him for the Apple store. Or for the Rothschild Modern, for that matter. At least, I didn't want to forgive him, though how could I hold anything against him? I looked at him and sighed. Then I looked around anxiously, wondering who in the street had watched me get frisky with Brian on the Internet.

What had possessed us to try all those positions?

I really wished I'd been back at the gym for the last few months instead of vegetating at home in front of Netflix. But everyone wore the blank, unscathed faces of innocence, and I calmed myself. I mean, the video of Brian and me wasn't on YouTube or anything. It was on an art gallery website. How many people were really interested in art anymore when work and family and texting and tweeting and Facebook and TV and real Internet porn competed for their time and attention?

Likely, Cliff was right, and my appearance in the video was neither original nor particularly memorable. It kind of perked me up to think of myself as bad in bed. When all else failed, at least I had that.

"Right through here," Brian said, waving me

through the tall black gates to Columbia Campus. "We don't want to be late."

Then he was race-walking me past the busts of Zeus, Apollo, and Athena in the entryway, and into the Rotunda at Low Memorial Library. We moved through groups of students who streamed into the elegant hall, which was not a library, and which arched high overhead, a gorgeous dome patterned after the Pantheon in Rome.

I would have drifted off into images of Rome and classical art, but I glanced at the stage and what I saw froze me in my tracks. Not what—who.

Brian.

How was that possible when Brian stood next to me, clutching my arm, and chuckling? "Oh ye of little faith," he said, dragging me toward a seat.

"But, but, but," I stuttered. "That's you."

He pressed his mouth against my ear. "That's me in this world. I'm me from mine. We're the same, but we're not."

I gawked and took in the crowds who had come to hear Dr. Brian Tennyson's lecture. "His books must be something if he can pull in this big an audience!"

Brian winced. "So he's a little more successful than I am. But he didn't get to love you, and I did. So I say that I came out ahead."

This professor was really packing them in. He must be a superstar in the physics world. I murmured, "Relationships are great, so is success."

"Says the pot to the kettle. At least I had a relationship. All you have is old people." Brian pushed me into the row, muttering apologies to other seated folks. We got center positions near the front, which seemed to please him.

"My eldercare work is very fulfilling," I argued sotto voce.

"Maybe. But not like a good marriage." He leaned into me. "You forget that I invented a device to traverse parallel worlds. His books are nice, but my achievement is huge. We're talking Nobel Prize huge."

"Shh," I said because the other Brian was smiling and waving to the audience. He certainly was cute, polished to a fine sheen and slicked up like a rock star. The Brian goofiness was toned down and the Tennyson intelligence stood out in high relief. Then the lights dimmed.

The President of Columbia introduced him, and then Professor Tennyson of this world spoke for an hour and a half about the cosmos and time and mirror symmetry and something called strings which allowed the universe to tear apart. It made approximately no sense to me, except that I was mesmerized by the doppelgänger effect. The man on stage was a mirror image of the one sitting beside me, and it was all happening before my eyes, though I was the only one who knew it.

Was it possible that Brian had been telling the truth this whole time?

What about Ofee's information?

Professor Tennyson called for questions. Brian's hand shot up.

"Yes, you there," Professor Tennyson smiled graciously at Brian.

"Professor Tennyson, this is all most impressive, you've done your homework on mirror symmetry. Here's a question, what's your take on the many worlds interpretation?" asked Brian, affecting a clipped British accent.

Professor Tennyson shrugged. "Hm. Well, it's sexy, no question. But it denies the actuality of wave-function collapse."

Brian stood up. "You can't believe that reality is a single unfolding history. And Everett did remove the postulate of wave-function collapse from the theory. Brilliant work really."

"Schrödinger's equation always applies. A fine invocation of Occam's razor," Professor Tennyson nodded. "Of course, if you remove wave-function collapse from the quantum formalism, then you need to derive the Born rule. Though Deutsch did good work on that front."

"Exactly!"

"Perhaps we'll take the next question," interjected the President of Columbia.

"One more question, if I may." Brian threaded his way out of the row to the aisle. He flicked the long blond hair over his shoulder. "Let's talk Level III multiverse."

A feeling of horror crept over me, and I beckoned quietly for Brian to return to his seat. Four hundred people were watching him, and maybe the two Brians weren't supposed to come together, like matter and anti-matter, or Clark Kent and Superman, or peanut butter and tuna fish. My Brian ignored me.

Professor Tennyson looked intrigued. "If space is finite, there are only finitely many multiverses at Level I but still infinitely many at Level III."

Brian beamed and gestured with both arms, like the conductor of an orchestra. "If space is infinite, there are infinitely many multiverses at both Level I and Level III, and just as many distinguishably different Level III as Level I multiverses."

"I really think other people in the audience—" started the President of Columbia. But he couldn't interrupt the two Brians, who were magnetically bonded to their conversation.

"Level IV is just crazy," said Professor Tennyson, staring at Brian.

"Absotively, posilutely nuts," Brian agreed, gesticulating. His fake accent had vanished from his speech.

"But please give me an alternative explanation of why we keep uncovering more and more mathematical regularity—" said the Professor.

"In the physical world!" both Brians chorused in identical voices. They beamed at each other.

"It begs the question," said Brian, "what did the nuclear physicist have for lunch?"

"Fission chips, of course," said Professor Tennyson. "Reminds me of the time two electrons were sitting on a bench in the park. Another electron walked by and said, 'Hey, can I come join you?'"

"The electrons said, 'Of course not, we're not bosons.' You know, I hear you are holding a seminar on time travel two weeks ago," Brian said. "I really want to go. I still might have."

Dr. Tennyson laughed. "Why did the chicken—"

"Gentlemen, this discussion is best continued after the Q and A," insisted the President of Columbia, firmly. "There are other members of the audience who would like to ask questions."

"Come back, right now!" I motioned again, more vehemently.

Professor Tennyson spied me, and his gaze crossed mine. He flushed scarlet from his collarbones to the widow's peak of his well-coiffed hair. "You!" he said, in a tone of pure horror.

I shielded my face with my hands and sank down in my seat.

Luckily a guy sitting behind me thought he was being called on, and he jumped up and asked a question about Planck length and supersymmetry.

Looking like the cat that had swallowed the eponymous bird, Brian slid in next to me. He put his hand on my shoulder and winked. "Now do you believe me?"

"Really, you had to call attention to yourself?" I whispered. "Now *he* noticed me. I think he saw the video, look how he keeps looking at me and blushing."

"Well, if he did, he ought to thank me, I've made him a sex symbol," said Brian, looking pleased with himself.

"He already was one to every female science nerd in the world," I muttered.

Brian flashed a hurt look at me. "Just because no one knows about my work on decoherence doesn't mean it's any less impressive. It's more impressive, really. We can go up and talk to him after the lecture. He's a fine fellow." Brian threw his arm around me and squeezed. "Then you know what we'll do?"

"I have no idea." The set of possibilities of what my Brian would do was literally infinite. I braced myself.

"The only thing you can do when you're broke, homeless, a rejected artist, and a porno star—"

"Who is in shock because there are two of you," I finished. Suddenly I felt a little brighter. I thought I knew where Brian was headed, and it was my kind of solution. "Get drunk?"

Brian grinned. "Get drunk and sing!"

Before the event ended, it came to me, in a moment of hyper-real clarity, what was really going on. The glossy, famous Professor was Brian's identical twin brother. Brian must have felt jealous of his twin, and made up the parallel worlds story when he had his psychotic break. It made me feel sorry for Brian, that he was so desperate for validation.

On pain of no more sex, I forbade him any more contact with the Professor—I didn't want to get entangled in a sticky family reunion—and dragged Brian out for that drink he'd promised me.

25 Justify my love

We hunkered in at the cheapest karaoke bar in the city, a grungy place on the Lower East Side, where I sat at a table littered with shot glasses.

Brian perched onstage, singing off-key, swiveling his hips out of rhythm with the Guns N' Roses anthem he was caterwauling. He was so bad that other patrons, classy as they were, and most of them were knuckle-draggers, stared in open-mouthed disbelief.

"I'm throwing a bottle at him," yelled a drunk man.

"Is this supposed to be funny, or is he just awful?" demanded a boozy woman.

"Look, he's serious," said a tipsy motorcycle enthusiast.

"Throw bottles!" yelled the first drunk man.

I jumped up and ran onstage. "Brian, you're great! Now it's my turn."

Brian grabbed me, dipped me, and kissed me passionately.

Whistles, catcalls, and cheers erupted. This was much more to the clientele's liking.

I should refer them to a particular art video.

I finally pushed Brian away, and he clasped his arms overhead victoriously. He leapt off the dais and jogged around, high-fiving our Neanderthal comrades. I turned to the Macbook Pro that sat on the speaker that controlled the music. I tapped in a song.

Might as well play the part. Sultry riffs of a favorite Madonna tune curled out into the air, and I unbuttoned my blouse to my cleavage, then tied it up around my midriff, exposing my tummy. In for a penny, in for a pound, right? Wasn't that always my motto?

Wasn't it time I had better mottos?

How drunk was I? I pushed away the nauseous feeling that was starting to curdle my gut. I was only about as good at drinking as I was in bed, which is, to paraphrase Cliff, enthusiastic but hackneyed.

The music streamed on, and I ran my fingers through my hair, fluffing it up into a wild mane. "I wanna kiss you in Paris, I wanna hold your hand in Rome. I wanna run naked in a rainstorm, make love in a train cross-country. You put this in me, so now what?"

At our table, Brian looked amazed. For once, I astonished him. Turnabout was fair play, right? It gave me a wicked thrill and prompted me to even more lascivious movement. I swayed my hips, writhed, and pulsed.

The audience screamed. They loved me.

Brian's eyes widened.

"What are you gonna do? Talk to me, tell me your dreams, am I in them?" I sang.

The crowd roared in approval. Maybe I had been too harsh on them. Weren't they all just adorable?

Brian jumped out of his chair and ran out of the bar.

26 Save yourself (Brian in this world)

Brian paced on the dark street. Tessa, weaving and unsteady, came out toward him.

"Brian, sup?" she slurred.

"That song means something to me and you in my world," he told her. Remembering what it meant made him hurt all over again, made him feel the constant familiar ache of loss and loneliness. He was reminded again that he was bereft, not just of his wife, but also of his foundational faith in the goodness of things. He swallowed. "That's, like, our song."

She giggled. "It can still be our song." She broke into a lilt. "I wanna kiss you in Paris . . . ."

What the hell was wrong with her? Couldn't she see he had feelings? Didn't she understand what he'd been through? "God, Tessa, you're more sensitive in my world."

"Nope, not anymore," she said, pronouncing

her words with exaggerated care. "I'm dead in your world. 'Member? Do you see dead people? Whoooo. Boo!" She danced and chuckled. Then her cell phone rang.

"Ofee! I love you. Kisses, hugs," she hollered as if Ofee was hard of hearing.

Then she dropped the phone and swayed.

Brian grabbed up the phone and placed it in Tessa's hand. She curled her fingers around it and accidentally pressed the speaker button.

"Tessa, I had to call you. I remembered something about that guy you asked about," said Ofee.

Brian had a strong impression of Ofee pretzelled up in an impossible yoga pose with his foot holding the phone.

"Brian, he's crazy, but he's some kinda sexy." Tessa leered at Brian, who suddenly felt queasy.

"Tessy, listen, he's crazier than you know. Norma said that when they took the guy away, his apartment was filled with thousands of photos of some woman he was stalking. He wrote essays about sick things he wanted to do to her."

"What?" Brian demanded. "That's not me! I'm not a psycho killer—"

"Is that him?" Ofee yelled. "Tessy, save yourself!"

"Brian, tell me the truth," Tessa said. She scrunched up her face with excessive ferocity. "Do you have an identical twin brother? And how long did you follow me before I saw you that day across the street?"

Brian would have answered, but Tessa suddenly looked distressed and unsteady on her feet. She dropped her phone onto the ground, and it hung itself up.

"Brian," she moaned. She vomited on him, then pitched forward into his arms.

Brian struggled to hoist her over his shoulder. He grunted, trying to position her correctly.

"The end is not the contemplation of something beautiful, but an experience of a carnal and primitive sort," said a voice behind him.

Brian turned slowly. "Guy. What are you doing here?"

"I want the piece." Guy slinked up to him from the shadows. "I have a buyer lined up."

"Tell your buyer to stand down."

Guy took out his knife and stared at it reverently. He tested the edge with his thumb and nodded in satisfaction. "No one backs away from a deal I have set up. There are no second chances."

"There are always second chances," Brian said. He staggered a little, shifting Tessa so that her chin didn't bang onto his shoulder blade. "We need some time."

"She is traversed by a double caesura. Your pretty girlfriend needs her thumb for her work. I know that from experience."

"I don't have a girlfriend, I'm faithful to my wife!" snapped Brian.

"You will have to surrender before the syncretism and the absolute and unstoppable polytheism of consequences. We all do." Guy's eyebrows rose and he shrugged with far more eloquence than he would ever achieve with words. "I want it. By tomorrow. Or else."

27 The music of Kol Nidre is beautiful in Brian's other worlds

It was a typical university ghetto apartment for assistant professors, the kind of shoddy, dilapidated apartment that always made Brian wish he could do better than this. His wife deserved so much more. He should be able to give her more, to give her the rich, elegant life she deserved. He just didn't work as much as he should because he preferred to spend his time with her. His research went unattended, and, if he was honest with himself, even his teaching was perfunctory.

He stood watching her as she practiced the cello. She was beautiful and peaceful, mellow and self-assured as she played the melancholic strains of Kol Nidre, penance and atonement, ends and beginnings.

The phone rang. Brian jumped and hurried to their closet-sized kitchen to answer it. A brisk professional voice asked for Tessa. He felt the call was important, so he crossed over to her with phone in hand.

"Tessa, sorry to interrupt when you have the synagogue tomorrow night."

Her face lit up with the sparkle he loved. "Yes, a paying gig," she said.

"The synagogue is lucky to get you. It's the doctor's office. You need to take this. Sounds serious."

Tessa carefully settled her cello and bow. She caught sight of his face and giggled. "You worry too much, silly professor. I have some pesky virus, that's all."

She kissed Brian, a casual and affectionate kiss that bespoke both their years together and the endless years ahead. She took the phone from him with a smile.

The bow of her cello flew off the chair of its own accord, a dark wing clinging to the air before clattering in slow motion to the floor.

Brian had a sudden, heartrending intuition.

28 Papier maché (Brian again, yet, still, and more)

Brian settled Tessa on Ofee's futon. She wore a clean T-shirt, and he wiped her face with a towel and stroked her hair away from her cheeks.

How could she look so much like his wife, but be so different? She was so messy and all over the place. His Tessa was more composed.

At least it was still Tessa.

Brian's clothes were sodden with vomit. He shucked them off and slid in next to her. He wrapped his arms around her still form, unable to resist squeezing her. She groaned.

"Please don't throw up on me," Brian murmured. "I just want to hold you like I used to."

Tessa snored in response.

Brian remembered the many times he'd curled up around his wife, feeling her sweet, solid form against him, making everything right, proving that the universe was as fundamentally good as he thought it was.

Would he ever feel that way again?

Brian was achy and wakeful as he held Tessa. If only he could hold *his* Tessa one more time. Things would be so much better. He might even be okay.

Her cell phone rang. Brian groaned but swung himself out of bed and grabbed it off the nightstand. "Hello?"

"Is this Brian? Where's Tessa?" demanded Frances Gates.

"Frances, how's it going?" Brian said. "I'm still thinking about that great suit. It's ridonculously awesome."

"Thank you, Brian, you're a doll. But let me speak to that woman who stole my Cliff Bucknell skull. You promised I'd have it by now. I want my piece."

"Listen, about that, there's something you should know."

"There's nothing for me to know, Brian. I want the piece by noon tomorrow, or else I'm calling the police. This is a business matter!" Frances hung up.

Brian stared hard at Tessa in bed. Frances wouldn't be denied; neither would Guy. He yawned and stretched, walked over to the kitchen area, and rifled through Ofee's drawers and cupboards.

29 Art lite, decaffeinated

At least the room wasn't still spinning. The futon condescended to hold still, too. I pulled myself up to a seated position and cradled my head in my arms. A few moments of moaning pitifully, and I was ready to stand. Almost.

Brian sat hunched over at Ofee's table. He was working on something and wearing a too-small T-shirt. He smelled acrid with undertones of vetiver and vomit, or was that just the soggy pile of clothes by the bed?

"There's nothing here with caffeine," I remembered.

"Yeah, I looked. Is Ofee allergic?" Brian asked.

"Philosophically opposed. Oh, I think I'm going to die."

"Not funny," Brian muttered.

I giggled, though it was painful. "Oops." I sat down opposite Brian and saw what he was working on: two lumpy papier maché objects. After some focusing, my gritty, burning eyes recognized them as skulls. A bowl of water and a book from which strips had been torn sat on the table at Brian's elbow.

"My mother said there was no right way or wrong way to do this, but I'm beginning to wonder."

"Skulls?" I asked.

"Guy showed up last night after you passed out. His knife looks sharp. And Frances called. He's a little mad that he hasn't got his skull back. Actually, he's a lot mad. I want him to cool down. Guy, too. I want you to be safe." Brian made a concerned face at me. His eyes were circled with black rings and sunk deep in his head and his hair was even more bedraggled than ever. He hadn't slept much, though I vaguely remembered him being in bed with me.

It hurt my fuzzy brain to think. "How'd Frances get my number?"

"I told him," Brian said, with a 'duh' grin. "It never occurred to me that you wouldn't give his art back."

Oh. I scowled and tried to focus. Were my eyes crossing or just watering? "These won't fool Guy or Frances."

"They're not supposed to," Brian said. "We'll pass them off as other, new Cliff Bucknells."

"I thought you were against forgery."

"I am. But I'm also for my wife. I don't agree with what you did, but if you're in a jam, I have to help you out. Think these are worth a million dollars?"

"No," I shook my head. I felt my eyes water for real, and tears leaked down my face. "Yes! This is the sweetest thing anyone's ever done for me!" I jumped up and hugged him. Naturally, he groped my ass. I didn't mind. "I don't even mind that you're a crazy stalker who has an identical twin brother and who's planning to murder me and drop my severed body parts into the Hudson River."

Brian sighed. He wriggled out of my grasp and perused me. "Tessa, we have to talk about your fantasy life. It's going down some negative paths. Don't model your universe that way. Choice plays an important role in macroscopic decoherence."

I kissed the top of his scruffy head. "You're crazy but wonderful. Here, if you don't mind, let me fix these. My hands are itching to take over."

By midday, I knew I still had it: my old skill as a mimic of other people's bad art. I had never wanted such a talent and didn't prize it, but it remained with me, like a cold sore on my upper lip or a terrible perm in my hair.

The two skulls now looked like real modern *objets d'art*. They were covered in glitter, with gaping eyes made of cat's-eye marbles. We'd found glitter, marbles, and other artsy odds and ends at Ofee's.

Brian gawked, amazed. "You're going to be just fine–you're talented. These look like the real thing. I couldn't make anything this good. Not in any universe."

"You can't sing or do magic either." I smiled as I continued to refine the skulls. My fingers moved expertly over the faces.

Brian pretended to pout. "Meanie."

"Sap."

"Sadist."

"Martyr."

"Martyr?" He looked wounded.

"What's the word for reveling in your own pain and suffering?" I couldn't attend to our banter when I was making a masterpiece. Two of them.

"Masochist, and I'm not one of those!"

"Please." I snorted. "You're in love with your wife's deadness. The dead wife you invented in an imaginary world, maybe because your identical twin brother is a superstar and you needed to feel important."

"There's nothing imaginary about my feelings. It hurts to lose someone you love," Brian said with heat. "It hurts so bad you can't imagine. Sometimes I can't breathe. The days without you stretch out like an unending wasteland, gray and empty forever. All our plans and dreams for our life died with you. I only ever wanted to be with you from the moment I met you. If you loved David here the way I love you there, you'd understand."

I surveyed the two skulls. Behold: they are good. Maybe, just possibly, they might buy me, if not redemption, then some time to figure things out.

I glanced up at Brian and saw that my T-shirt matched his, except that it fit me better. I poked him in the chest. "You couldn't find something else for me to wear?" I teased. "We have to be yoga twins?"

"I packed a negligee for you, but it didn't seem appropriate last night." His voice was still raw and his gaze was averted.

"I have a negligee?"

"Back of the pajama drawer."

"I loved David," I said, and the old pang of loss and regret reverberated in my chest like a gong. I placed the two skulls on a window shelf under a hanging crystal pendant to dry. "I built my world around him. But even before he left, our marriage was limping along. I couldn't figure out how to fix it. I used to dream that I needed David desperately, but I couldn't get my phone to work to call him. I'd wake up in a panic, crying. When he left, I had to face it. That everything between us had long ago come to an ignominious stop. That was a kind of death—the death of my dreams and illusions, anyway." I ran my fingers over one of the skulls, patting down the silver glitter where it had clumped. "Two skulls, one for Frances, one for Guy. Smart. You're really smart, Brian."

Brian came up behind me and hugged me, but loosely. "One of your drawings shows two people walking away from each other, going to a party or a wake, it could be either, there's a sense of possibilities."

"They're not going to a party. Oh, forget it!" I turned around to look into his eyes. It was a dislocated moment of déjà vu because of having shared so much in such a short time. And underlying everything was that odd sense of familiarity, but did we really know each other? I suppose we were still feeling each other out.

"Want to model the negligee?" Brian asked in a thick voice, trying to be playful.

"I would." I felt a pang of disappointment, and I kissed the tip of his nose lightly. "But I have to go to work. There's a ton of stuff to do for the dance tonight."

"Some thanks I get for saving your ass," he muttered, stepping back.

"I heard that. Speaking of bare asses, don't think I couldn't feel you in bed last night."

"You barfed on my clothes." Brian gave me a wry look.

"Not on your underwear."

"I was kamikaze when I went through the decohering device."

"Kamikaze?"

"No undies," he explained.

I laughed. In that moment, I also believed. I don't know why that moment broke open the locked gate of my inner impasse and ushered me into a magical world of faith. So maybe there was no identical twin brother. Maybe it was exactly as Brian said: he had come from a parallel world to find me. Occam's razor, right? The simplest explanation. The explanation that gave a new luster to everything, especially my heart. "You went through a radical physics invention not wearing underwear?" Only Brian.

"Underwear was optional; the math wasn't. I have to take a nap, but I'll bring the skulls to you when they dry."

"They're not bad," I told him. "They just might do the trick."

30 The impression of infinite vastness

The afternoon was a blur of activity at the Collegiate Church. I helped volunteers hang crepe-paper streamers and set up tables with baked goods. I climbed a ladder and strung up a million-faceted silver disco ball. We swept and polished and sent emails reminding folks to come.

Brian arrived with a box around dinner time. We placed the box in my office and then helped ourselves to Pellegrino water, cupcakes, and zucchini bread.

After snacking and fussing some more, I went into a bathroom to change. I came out wearing a strappy black silk camisole and fluttery silk skirt. I'd forgotten I owned such a girly flirtatious outfit; Brian had packed it for me in the suitcase, and I'd stuck it in my messenger bag to bring to the dance.

Chad and Jordan trooped in with a group of Apple store workers. I was overcome with embarrassment but squared my shoulders and raised my chin defiantly. I refused to let myself succumb to the old, familiar bad feelings. At some point, I had to cut them loose. It seemed easier to do so with Brian staring at me open-mouthed.

"Dr. Tennyson," Jordan called.

But Brian was mesmerized by me. "Wow, Tessa, you look beautiful! I hate seeing you in those shapeless work clothes. You look like a banker, not like you."

Reverend Pincek joined us. "You do look lovely tonight, Tessa." He beamed and then went off to greet guests, who were streaming in after paying admission to Joan and other volunteers at the door.

The Apple store geniuses swarmed around us, though all Brian and I could see were each other.

"Hi, Dr. T, Tessa. No flying shoes tonight, hey? Maybe another video, haha? That first one's had over two million hits on YouTube."

"I dropped by the store this afternoon and invited them," Brian said to me as if they weren't present. "I figured your church needed the money."

"We brought copies of your book to sign, Dr. T," Chad said.

That roused Brian from his reverie of me. "Sure. I'll sign breasts, too, especially perky ones."

The geniuses laughed and clustered eagerly

around Brian, who joked and bantered and signed their books.

Big band music burst out over the loudspeakers. People of all ages filled the floor: little kids jamming with awkward childish grace, teens, adults, even Mr. James shuffling on his walker and bopping his head.

More people lined up outside the doors, waiting to pay and enter.

The evening was a success, no question. It felt like my first victory in a long, bleak while, and I relished it. I breathed it all in: the social hall with people milling and dancing, the colored streamers, the flashing lights of the disco ball . . . FLASH: a painting. *A room with a faceted glowing orb at the center, strewn light, and dancing figures. Two walls opened onto a magical mountainscape, and a man and a woman twirled off together on a beautiful, high crest. He looked like Brian, and the whole wondrous image was reminiscent of Chagall.*

Chagall?

"Hey, Dreamy, how about this dance?" It was Brian, and I hadn't even noticed him approaching. He gathered me into his arms.

"You won't take no for an answer." I snuggled closer in to him.

"Never do, when it comes to you." Gracefully, he swayed with me in a neat box step.

"I don't know how to dance this way."

"Let me lead. For once," he answered dryly.

I was softening into him when I felt someone staring. The hair on the back of my neck rose and pulsed. I looked around and spied a lone figure leaning back against the wall, smoking. "Guy's here," I whispered to Brian.

Brian stiffened and then released me. "Show time."

We made our way through the crowds of people to Guy. He grabbed me roughly. "Where is it? I want it now!"

"You're hurting me," I said, straining away from him.

"Let her go," Brian barked. "We've got it." He motioned.

Guy dragged me to follow Brian. We all went into my eldercare office. Guy closed the door balefully.

I reached into the cardboard box and gently pulled out one of the skulls. "Here."

"*Voilà*, a Cliff Bucknell skull!" Brian said with a flourish.

Guy stared and turned the skull over and over in his hands. His roughhewn face softened a smidgen, and I thought he was going to accept the skull. "What shakes our spirit is not the impression of infinite vastness, but of infinite power." He smashed the skull down on my desk. He pummeled it. Quick as quanta, he grabbed my right hand and pinned it to my desk. He raised his knife.

I screamed. No one could hear me over the music.

Brian launched himself atop Guy. "Wait! It's in her apartment!"

Guy shook Brian off the way a bear would shake off a small dog, then kicked him. "What's it doing there?"

"I'm locked out," I cried. "I'm broke. I haven't paid my co-op bill in years."

Guy made an ugly piffle of disgust. "Even with a neo-Pythagorean return to the aesthetics of proportion and number that works against current sensibilities, you were never going to be a good enough artist to make money selling your paintings. "

"I thought I had talent. I guess I was just fooling myself."

"Your talent is forging. I know, I move art all the time." Guy kicked Brian a few more times when Brian tried to get up, then Guy placed his foot heavily on Brian's chest.

"I don't want to be a forger!" I cried. "I want more than that."

"You have a little talent for porn. I found you tame, personally," Guy shrugged. "Sentiments are not merely a perturbation of the mind, but express, together with reason and sensibility, a third faculty of humankind."

"I'm not a porn star, I'm an artist." I was weeping hard now, big gulps of tears and snot that shook my whole body.

"You'll be a forger without thumbs if you don't get me that skull. Now."

"I don't know what to do anymore," I said brokenly. "Everything I try fails. Maybe you *should* just cut off my thumbs. Maybe I deserve it after everything I've done. Making that stupid skull and all Cliff's other pieces while he was sick. Posing for the Warhol tribute. David was right to leave me. I was so stupid."

"Have it your way," Guy said. He raised his knife.

Brian squirreled around under Guy's foot and freed himself, then leapt to hold Guy's arm. "No! Now is not the time for you to give up, Tessa!" He and Guy wrestled for Guy's knife.

"What do you want from me?" I wailed.

Guy swatted Brian, who flew like a ragdoll across the tiny office, hitting the wall with a resounding thud. Guy laughed and gripped my hand. "I want thumbs to add to my collection. Or the original Cliff Bucknell skull, even if you're the one who made it."

"Tessa, think, come on," Brian croaked, holding his ribs.

"We'll break into my apartment and get the skull!"

Guy considered. He released my hand but clutched my elbow painfully.

Brian led as we walked out my office and through the music and masses toward the door. I swiped at my tearstained face with the back of my hand.

Brian's head tilted suddenly. He swiveled around and grabbed a big-brimmed hat off one of my old ladies. Then he dropped back behind us, hunching down.

Guy's eyes narrowed and he scrutinized the room, keeping a firm hold on my arm.

I squirmed in Guy's relentless grasp, trying to see what had prompted Brian to act so strangely at the most ghastly, inopportune occasion possible.

The next moment, Professor Brian Tennyson passed.

"Brian!" I exclaimed.

"Yes?" chorused the two Brians.

But Guy hurtled me forward, through the door.

I struggled to look back over my shoulder.

My Brian, always one to seize the moment, pulled down the veiled brim of the borrowed hat and stepped up to the professor. "Might I say, sir, how brilliant you are? Not only brilliant, but also handsome. A quick word: metric tensors in macroscopic decoherence."

"I've been noodling around on that but I've been too busy with book tours and rock climbing—" started Professor Tennyson.

"Get your priorities straight," barked my Brian. "Love is what matters!" Those words seemed to invigorate him, as spinach did Popeye. Testosterone up and spoiling for a fight, he swung back around toward Guy and me.

But flashing lights cut off the moment. Siren wailing, a cop car pulled up. Guy ran me around it and bundled me into a taxi. Brian raced toward us, but the taxi took off with a squeal.

31

WD-40 makes the sublime slippery

I pushed open the door. A file, a set of picks, and a can of WD-40 sat on the floor beside me. "It's my apartment. I own it. They can't keep me out without a court order and a sheriff. I won't let them."

Brian rushed up, panting. "Tessa, how'd you get in?"

I didn't answer. Brian was a quick study; he'd figure it out. I felt a surge of new determination as I carefully peeled the painted-over eviction notice off the door.

"The rational upshot of the experience of the sublime is the recognition of the independence of human reason from nature. That is to say, Tessa helped Bucknell with all kinds of things," Guy chuckled. "She has skills."

"Tessa, did you burgle art you had forged?" Brian asked, dismayed. "I don't even know who you are anymore!"

I was about to give Brian a stiff answer. Of course I never burgled. But I had picked Cliff's lock at his apartment in Soho and at his studio in the Catskills and even, memorably, at his beach house in East Hampton when he was too high to get himself home safely. But then my cell phone rang. I answered it without thinking.

Guy laid a warning hand on my shoulder. He needn't have worried; it wasn't the kind of call that could save me from this situation. My body recoiled from the blow and my eyes closed. I murmured numbly and hung up. "That was Reverend Pincek. Mrs. Leibowitz died."

"Who cares about some old lady?" snarled Guy. "Art is what matters. Get me the fucking million-dollar skull."

A moment later, I did just that. It was in my kitchen cabinet exactly where Brian had said it would be. I pulled it out and it winked at me, as if acknowledging our old secrets. I handed it to Guy.

Guy took a last drag from his cigarette and then flicked it into my sink. He never took his eyes off the skull. "I have a buyer who'll pay $200K. Our old arrangement, Tessa, you get half. Though you've caused me so much trouble, I should impose a pain and suffering tax."

"That's blood money," Brian said fiercely.

"What limitation can prevent not only the reduction of things but also of people to the level of objects that can be manipulated, exploited, modified, or quantified?" asked Guy.

"It's art money," I said wearily. "It doesn't mean anything. It has nothing to do with how good the art is."

Just then, a pounding sounded at the front door.

"NYPD, open up!" ordered a stentorian voice.

Guy slipped the skull into a bag, ran to the living room window, and climbed out.

I grabbed Brian's arm. "Brian, you go, too!"

"I have to take care of you," he demurred.

"I can take care of myself."

The pounding got louder. I dragged Brian to the window.

"Whoa, we're four floors up? I never learned how to climb, and force equals mass times acceleration. If I fall—"

But I wasn't going to pander to him. He had to leave, now, that was what was best for him. And I always knew what was best for other people. "There are big hand-holds all the way down. Decohere yourself out that window, Professor!" I shoved.

Brian scrambled out. He took a last pleading look over the ledge at me. "My wife would never push me out the window."

"For the last time, I'm not your wife!" I snapped.

I took the painting off the table. I ran to the bedroom, threw open a drawer and found another piece of paper, written and signed by none other than Cliff Bucknell. I rolled the two pieces of paper together and slid the narrow tube inside the waistband of my skirt. Then I ran back and opened the door to two of New York's finest.

"Tessa Barnum? You are under arrest for the theft of valuable merchandise from the Gates Gallery. You have the right to remain silent . . . "

As they snapped handcuffs around my wrists, I consoled myself with the thought that they had called it merchandise, and not art.

32 The oldest profession: forgery

I sat in a holding cell with a trio of hookers. They were eying me with interest. I eyed them back with equal curiosity. Somehow, incredibly, given the situation, I felt buoyant. I was a little sad and a little angry, but mostly I was more alive and more determined than I had felt in years.

The first hooker, wearing fishnets, a pleather mini-skirt, and a tube top, said, "You must be high class. Whaddya get, a thousand bucks a night?"

"I'm in here for taking art," I said.

She giggled. "Is that a new name for it? Fancy! How much do you get?"

"I took a piece of art. Literally."

Hooker number two, who sported an Adam's apple and extravagantly feminine curves showcased by a black spandex catsuit, had been staring quizzically for the last hour. A light broke on her face.

"I know you. You're the Internet porn girl with the tattoo on her ass!"

"My sacrum," I said. "It's not a tattoo."

The third hooker, dressed in a slinky gold frock, sat upright on the bench. "Yeah, that's you. Didn't see much of your face in that YouTube video, because of all the different positions, but now I recognize you. Did you raise your prices after that?"

Fishnets winked at me. "Great location for a tattoo. Very sexy."

"It's a birthmark. Above my ass. Not on it."

"You're too good to have a tattoo on your ass?" demanded Slinky Gold Frock, defiantly. The other two murmured things about my snobby attitude.

I laughed shortly. If only they knew. "I'm not good enough to have a tattoo on my ass." That quieted them.

"You have a great ass," said Adam's Apple, after a few minutes. "I need to do something about mine. It's huge."

Now I couldn't help but smile sadly. Didn't I just have this conversation? "Your ass is perfect," I assured Adam's Apple, earnestly. "A friend of mine says men like big asses. I think she was right."

"Thanks honey," she said.

"I'm going to make my ass bigger," decided Fishnets. "Your ass really did look all plump and fine in the video. Did it get you more business?"

"The Internet thing was an accident."

"No such thing as accidents, honey," said Adam's Apple.

"I don't think the video would get me more business, if I was in that business," I mused with my old sense of deflation. "I think it showed me as, well, enthusiastic and idealistic, but hackneyed. Not very good in bed."

The ladies giggled.

"Are you kidding?" asked Fishnets. "That's all you need."

"Ninety percent of what men want in bed is enthusiasm," added Adam's Apple confidentially. "The other ten percent is head."

I gave her a hard look. "Are you sure? I always think there's some secret skill that other women have that I don't." *Some secret skill in bed, some secret skill in life*, I thought, but didn't say aloud.

"Trust me," Adam's Apple said. "Enthusiasm and head."

"Trust yourself more," said Fishnets. "Don't be so self-conscious. Just go for it."

The other two liked that advice and murmured similar comments.

Frances Gates stormed up to the cell. Today he wore a turquoise suit of nubby raw silk to go with his expression of outrage and indignation. He glared at me. "I can't believe you'd call me, of all people, to bail you out. I'm the one who wants you in jail!"

I gripped the bars. "You want to hear what I have to say. Frances, I have legal claim to that head. I have a letter in Cliff's writing stating that I made it under his auspices and that he gives it to me."

Frances emptied out like a balloon with the helium released. "I hate forgers."

"But I have a proposition for you," I continued.

"Honey, he ain't interested in your proposition," Adam's Apple said. "You got a brother?"

The girls chortled. I stifled a grin and shushed them. I turned back to Frances. "I can get you a head."

"I want my head," wailed Frances, looking woebegone.

"Remember, they all want head," called Fishnets. "It cheers them up."

More giggles. I waved at them: did they mind? I was having an important conversation. I was, after all, following their advice: I was going for it. "Frances, do you remember three years ago, the rumors about Bucknell forgeries? During his breakdown."

Frances looked like he was about to cry, but he was wary, at the same time. "I remember he had a breakdown."

"I was his student then. The pseudo-Warhol prints. I'm the model. Look at me. Don't you recognize me?"

Frances leaned close to the bars and perused me. Slowly his face changed.

"I was the forger, too." I sighed. "When he couldn't get out of bed. I didn't mean to be. But Cliff was incapacitated. It ripped out my heart to see him that way. I was trying to save him, to get him back on his feet. So I finished his commissions."

"I heard all this wild gossip," Frances mused. "No one was ever sure which of his pieces were forgeries. I mean, his style is distinct."

"He has no style," I cried before I could stop myself. I banged my head against the bars. "Argh! That's the point. It's ugly derivative crap."

Frances uttered a sound of disgust and swiveled on his heel and sashayed away.

"Better talk to him about head again," said Fishnets. "If you want him to stay."

"Wait, Frances, please," I cried.

He paused and tapped his foot, then stared at the time on his iPhone.

"What if you do a show about me, as Cliff's model, student, forger, and protégé."

"A show about you?" Frances snorted.

"His influence on me. You have the Warhol prints. I'll remake the skull. And I have photographs of the other forgeries. It can also be an exposé on the forgeries."

Frances stepped closer. "How would you recreate the head?"

"Same way I did it in the first place," I said, shrugging. "Sculpt it in clay, make a mold, cast it in resin. Patina it and glue on the rhinestones with Elmer's."

"I couldn't get a million dollars from that." Frances looked doubtful.

"You'd get a million dollars worth of PR," I noted, baiting the hook. "Worldwide attention. Cliff is an international figure. There was a lot of gossip about the forgeries. Everyone was titillated and appalled at the same time. Viciously appalled." I winced. "I found that out the hard way."

Frances bit. "I would be the gallery who revealed the untold secrets."

"It's a great angle," I sang. "Everyone would cover it, general media and arts media. *Vogue*, *Arts and Antiques*, *W*, *Fine Art Connoisseur*, *American Arts Quarterly*, the morning show . . . "

Frances' face actually paled with glee. "People would come from everywhere to visit the gallery."

"People would talk about it for years. You'd be famous."

"Not famous. Infamous." Frances smiled. "I always wanted to be infamous."

"You would show my work, too," I said, lightly, but pointedly and carefully.

"Ugh. Everyone's an artist. Sorry, sister, no. That I can not do." Frances made a dismissive hand motion.

I reached under my skirt, which brought a chorus of approval from the girls, and pulled out the rolled-up papers. I passed them through the bars to Frances.

Frances made a moue of impatience, but he opened them up. First he saw the handwritten letter from Cliff, and he was crest-fallen all over again. He kind of moaned.

Then he saw the painting. His head lifted and his eyebrows raised and the light of dawning pleasure radiated over his face.

So help me God, homeless, broke, discredited, starring in Internet porn, and locked up in jail, I had the best moment of my entire life right then: seeing Frances captivated by my painting.

It was worth everything I'd been through just to see the true pleasure on his face as he beheld my work.

"You did this?" Frances asked with some disbelief. "Oil on paper?"

"Oil on eviction notice," I clarified.

"Turner influence," he noted. "Interesting use of color. Almost old masterish, in a good way, the palate. Florentine. But absolutely contemporary, too."

The ladies crowded around me, trying to see.

"I have dozens of canvases," I said. I was suddenly aflutter with nervousness and excitement. Was I really going to show my work to an important gallerist? Was I really setting up a show for myself? Was I really going for it, finally?

"All landscapes?"

"Yes. I have figure drawings, too. I always thought they were just doodles, but recently I was told they were good. They could be framed and shown."

"Hey, baby, let us see," pleaded Fishnets.

Frances held up the painting.

The girls fell silent, then oohed and aahed with admiration. They were now, officially, my new best friends.

Frances squinted at me fiercely, then shook his head and marched out.

I collapsed onto the bench and cradled my head in my arms. "Oh crap. Well, I tried."

"Honey, your painting's real good. He's coming back, you'll see," said Fishnets.

"You ain't a forger, you're an *artist*," said Adam's Apple reverently. "You should be proud."

But I was past that kind of pretension. I was just me, same ole screwed up Tessa, now jailed Tessa. "I'm a forger, all right. And a kind of art thief, sort of. I took something I shouldn't have, even if it was rightfully mine."

"I'd steal something beautiful like that," said Slinky Gold Frock. "Usually I only steal money from my guys, but I'd take that painting. It kinda gets you in the gut, makes you want to own it."

"Really?" I asked, gratefully. "You mean that?" It was one of the nicest things anyone had ever said about my work: that it elicited the lust for acquisition. They all three nodded.

"If you can paint something beautiful like that, what's all the commotion about the head and forgery?" asked Adam's Apple.

I slumped again. "That's the sad part. I can paint like that, and instead, I forged really, really ugly stupid crap. How pathetic is that?"

"We all done sad stuff," said Fishnets. "The

secret is to say you're sorry and make amends if you can. Then you shake it off and move forward as best you can."

• • •

A few hours later, Fishnets was painting my toenails while I sketched my new friends' faces on the cell wall with a tube of Nars Shanghai Red lipstick. The sketches were remarkably poignant, if I said so myself. The girls certainly did.

Adam's Apple wanted to take pictures of them and was hollering for her cell phone.

But when the cops returned, Frances trailed them. I dropped the lipstick and we all scrambled upright.

"Turns out there's a lot of paperwork when you drop charges," Frances said.

A police officer unlocked the holding cell door. "Come on, Picasso. You're sprung."

"Raphael, not Picasso!" I said. Then, because I couldn't help it, I pulled a Brian. I launched myself at Frances and squeezed him in a giant hug.

"Get off me," wheezed Frances. "There's no telling what diseases you picked up in there!"

"You won't regret this, I promise!" I said. "I'll make you lots of money."

"I'm taking 65 percent on your canvases, and all the profit on the new head," Frances said.

"Give him all the head he wants," called Adam's Apple.

I giggled. Then, because Brian would kill me if I didn't stand up for myself, I patted Frances and shook my head. "You can take 65 percent of the first couple of sales. Then we go to fifty-fifty. And you can take 60 percent of the head."

"First ten sales," Frances said. "Seventy-five percent of the head."

"First three," I responded. "Sixty-five percent."

"Five, sixty-five," he countered. We looked at each other and grinned, and then shook hands. "I am sorry about the original skull," he said with some regret. "Even if it does belong to you and I can't sell it. It was something special. I'd love to show it."

"Well, I do have an idea about how we might get it back," I drawled, having a flash of inspiration. For once, it was practical inspiration. I almost didn't recognize myself.

"Now you're talking," said Frances.

"I'll call Guy and say I've got a buyer willing to pay $750K. We'll set up a sting."

"More paperwork," rumbled the cop.

"I think I'm starting to like you," Frances said. "But don't breathe on me. Ugh."

"Bye, ladies," I waved. "Call me for those portraits. But I do have to charge you."

"No freebies," called Fishnets. There was a chorus of assents.

"I'll text you the name of the lady who waxes me," said Adam's Apple. "Your guy in the video will appreciate it. He seemed like a real sweetheart. Eager to make you happy, you know. He put your pleasure first. That would make anyone enthusiastic."

"Brian," I said. Where was he?

33 Channeling Tessa

He wasn't at my place, where I retrieved my cell phone. Nor was he at Ofee's apartment.

He wasn't at Central Park, which was lit up and full of people streaming toward a concert on the great lawn. He wasn't at Rat Rock.

He wasn't at Riverside Park. I was standing by the tree where I'd seen him hiding that day I walked Mrs. Leibowitz. Oh, Mrs. L. But I couldn't dwell on heartache right now.

Then my cell phone rang. It was Ofee, bursting with information that he just had to share with me immediately. But I already knew, because my heart knew.

"Ofee, I love you!" I said. "I know. It wasn't Brian Tennyson who took the pictures and wrote that stuff and was put away in an institution. It was some other professor. I figured that out."

But where would Brian go?

• • •

It came to me in a flash of obviousness once I stopped to think deeply about Brian. And I knew he was nearby because I could feel him as I ascended the steps to the great marble plaza at Lincoln Center, where masses of people milled about, surrounded by the Opera House, the theaters, the ballet halls, and Juilliard. The plaza was bathed in white lights. The scene was festive, lush, and vibrant.

There was Brian, a solitary observer of the panoply of people and traffic. A twinkly sphere of light seemed to play around him, distinguishing him from everyone else here in our world. Our rich, bursting, imperfect but wonderful world that was more beautiful because he had visited it.

I crossed over to sit next to him.

"She wanted to play here," he said, softly. He paused for a few beats. "She played at Carnegie. But she wanted to play here. The cultural institutions all in one place. It was a thing with her."

This was Brian: in love with his wife, that other Tessa. Not with me. With her, always her. It was bittersweet, and I felt a pang of sadness. But he had done so much for me that I wanted to help him. Maybe I could ease his sorrow. "You must have been so proud of her."

"Proud. Spellbound. Awed. I never told her how much. I told her I loved her, but I didn't really say how much she meant to me. That's why it's so hard to let go of her. I still have so much left to say to her." His eyes were suddenly shiny with a slick of tears.

I thought of his wife as I had glimpsed her that once, like a wraith in his aura: gaunt and dying in his arms. It must have been unimaginably painful for him. He had built his entire world around her.

He smeared at his eyes with the back of his hand.

All at once, because I was filled with new hope and new promise, I knew what to do for him. I stood. "I can help you with that."

Brian gave me a somber, quizzical look. "What do you mean?"

"You came to this world to see her again. To tell her one last time that you love her. That's why you followed me around."

"Yes, so?"

"So, I'll be her." I felt a connection to her, felt her nearby. "I'll be her right now. So you can say all the things you want to."

"Tessa, you're not my wife!"

"I look enough like her to play her," I said, smiling crookedly.

"She's a completely different person."

"I'll imagine who I'd be if I hadn't quit the cello and started drawing when I was twelve. If I'd succeeded in seducing my brother's tutor. If I'd gone to Yale instead of following David to Columbia." I would imagine myself after every decision that she had made until she slipped into me, like a hand taking on a glove.

Brian, sweet man, was imbued with native effervescence the way deep reds are saturated with blue. He rose to his feet, warming to the idea. "If you hadn't studied art but had come to New Haven and met me!"

"Ooh, that's a hard one: you or Renaissance art," I teased. "Just kidding. Give me a moment."

I stepped away, and passers-by instinctively gave us a wide berth. My eyes mostly closed, except for a thin slit. I imagined another life, other choices. It was easy for me because I spent so much time in my imaginal world. But the stakes were high—Brian's happiness—so I went deeper into it. I gave my whole being over to the exercise, every heartbeat.

A pale blue light shimmered around me. In transparency, like a ghost, another me, another Tessa, softer and more confident, stepped up beside me. I continued to concentrate on those other paths, the ones not taken.

My breathing deepened and slowed, and time

stopped. The blue light around me pulsed. It intensified. The space between heartbeats stretched into an eternity, and the other Tessa walked into my body. For a moment, we smiled at each other.

Then I stepped out.

"Hello, Professor," said Tessa, in a teasing voice.

Brian jumped. "Tessa! It's you!"

"Silly boy. I'm always around you," she said. "Always."

Brian grabbed her hands and clutched them to his chest. "Why did you leave?"

"It was my time. My life had run out, kind of like the joke at the end of a Haydn piece. The loud chord in the Surprise Symphony. You don't expect it, and there it is," she said, squeezing his hands back.

"It wasn't funny to me," Brian said raggedly.

"You always became humorless at just the wrong time."

"You're always so smug and sure you're right."

"Am I here to argue with you?" she asked with a fake yawn to show how boring that would be. "You know how that's going to end. I win, because I'm the superior wordsmith."

"I want you back to argue with me every day," Brian choked out. He put his arms around Tessa and held her tightly.

"I'm not coming back, Professor."

"But I love you, I love you so much." Brian's voice was raw, undefended.

"I know, and wasn't I good? I planned it that way." Tessa leaned her head to rest her cheek against Brian's.

"I was the one who chose you!"

"Silly. I knew you were going to love me the first day I saw you at Freshman Orientation." Tessa's laugh was silvery and sweet, as he remembered it.

"But you said we could only be friends. I thought I was the consolation prize because perfect David broke up with you."

"You were never second best, Brian. I wanted you. I wanted what we had. I love you, too. I always will. In every universe."

Brian couldn't speak. He struggled to hold in his tears but they spilled down his face. He clutched his Tessa to himself, feeling her every bone and muscle, every molecule, against his being. He engraved her into him. "You are the most amazing woman I ever met. The most amazing person."

"You don't have to say that. I already knew you felt that way."

"I miss you. I miss you every day. I miss holding you."

"I know. I feel your ache."

"What am I going to do without you?"

Tessa nodded against him. "Go on, and be happy. That's what I want. You to be happy. You know you always end up doing what I want."

"Always," Brian swore. He kissed her. For a long moment, or a half-hour, I was never sure which, they remained merged together, like two candlewicks into one flame.

"It's all good," she whispered. "We'll be together again." Then the other Tessa stepped out. She touched my hand briefly, and I felt her sweetness and lightness. Poor Brian, that he lost her. My heart swelled for him.

And for me, because I had to find a way to incorporate some of her into me.

"Thank you," she whispered. Then she was gone.

I was me again, incarnated.

"Oh! You're back," Brian said, releasing me.

"Sorry," I said, softly.

"No, no! God, Tessa, thank you. That was amazing. She was here. I felt her, I held her, I talked to her. My wife. My Tessa." His face was radiant, awestruck. The constant tension, like the tight boing of a spring, had eased from his body.

"I felt her, too. She's like me, but she's not me. She's herself," I said. "She's amazing. So sure of herself, but in a quiet way."

"My Tessa had a way of assuming that she was

right and would get whatever she wanted," Brian smiled and wiped his hand across his face.

"It didn't put you off."

"Nah, I knew she was a loon. A brilliant, sweet, sexy, nut case. Certifiable. I would look at her and think, 'I'm the one holding you.'"

"She was lucky to have you, Brian," I said wistfully, because I wondered, would anyone ever feel anything like that for me? David had been, well . . . imperious. Self-involved. If I was honest with myself about him. I had accommodated him because we had been together for so long that our history carried its own imperative. I repeated, "Yeah, she was lucky to have you."

"I know, right?" He laughed once, then stared off into the starlight. After a few moments, he said, "Actually, I was the lucky one. You go all through life, doing and performing and accomplishing, running like a gerbil on a wheel. I mean, I was a math star when I was ten. Teachers calling my parents, pressuring them to stick me in university early. 'Send him to Oxford, send him to Princeton.' Lucky for me, my mom's got a spine and some sense.

"My parents said no, he needs the social development with his peers. So, all the while I was getting educated, I was with people my own age. And that was lucky.

"Because if you're lucky, really lucky, you get to meet that one person who teaches you that all the doing and performing and accomplishing doesn't mean anything. Nada. Zero.

"What really matters is the non-physical, non-quantifiable thing, the feeling that when you're with her, you're more alive than you ever imagined possible. Even when it hurts. Even when she's gone."

I hugged Brian. "You'll love again."

"Maybe," he said softly.

"I wish it was going to be me."

Brian draped his arm around me in a friendly fashion and kissed my forehead. "I can't rule out another love anymore. Even if the ache lasts for a long, long time."

"Maybe it's supposed to," I said.

Brian nodded. "Next time, she'll have some bite to her. Like you. But she'll be just as kooky as you and my Tessa. I like being able to hold a woman. It makes me feel whole."

"What about holding me?" I asked, plaintively. "I'd really like that!"

Brian squeezed my shoulders gently. "You're not my Tessa. It's not my place."

34 Burnt eggs and Chagall

We went back to my apartment because I'd broken in, and because, after all, I hadn't been properly evicted. The final morning, after sleeping on my couch, Brian scrambled eggs. He burnt them but didn't pay attention, and I was too busy watching him and feeling forlorn to care.

"Hey, what's this package?" Brian asked. He lifted a parcel from my messenger bag.

"That's a gift from Mrs. Leibowitz. She said to open it after Saturday."

"Well, it's Sunday, so what are you waiting for?" he asked, cheerfully. He swirled the wooden spoon in the blackening eggs, a perfunctory motion. His gaze was focused on the package. "I love presents!"

"Me too," I said. I unwrapped the brown paper, pulled it away to reveal a small but exquisite Chagall painting of a nude woman on a dappled horse that was rising into the air. The woman held a paintbrush.

"Nice!" Brian exclaimed.

I was speechless. Finally, I said, "Nice? It's a Chagall."

"Real art?" Brian teased.

"Oh, yeah," I said, with a deep breath. "I don't know this piece, but the colors, poetic images and folk story-like ambience..."

"There's a note taped to the back," pointed Brian.

"'Dear Tessa, I hope this inspires you.'" I burst into tears. Brian patted my shoulder. "'And brings you many hours of pleasure. Thanks for all your time and care. Love, Mena Leibowitz. PS: Note her beautiful ass. Don't waste yours taking care of everyone but yourself.' Oh Brian."

"That lady had style! And she's absotively right about your ass." He winked at me, but it was like a brother, not like a lover.

"Isn't there any way for you to stay longer?" I asked.

"My time expires at 12:22. That's my limit."

"But who's going to appreciate my ass when you leave?" I was trying to be playful, but it came out mournful.

"You will, silly," he said. "I had my own Tessa. You have to find your Brian. Or Mark or Joe. I don't know who your destiny is here. There are so many possibilities. I think you should start enjoying them."

But I want you to be my destiny.

35 Beaming up

Just after noon, we sat shoulder to shoulder on a bench in a quiet part of Riverside Park. I tried to think of my life without Brian. It was hard to believe that so short a span of time, five days and four hours and twenty-two minutes, could leave an indelible mark on me.

I asked, "So, you'll go back to your world and what, publish a paper about your invention and win your world's Nobel Prize?"

"Nope. I'll write that book, *How the Enterprise Can Beam Us Up*. It's good. I'm smart here. But I'm smarter in my world. I can do an even better job." Brian looked eager to throw himself into the project.

"But you could be bigger than Einstein," I noted. "Your decoherence machine is, I mean, wow!"

"Look what they did with Einstein's work," he said softly. "Turned it into bombs. I'm destroying the device."

It seemed like a hugely irrevocable decision, but it was his to make. "I just found you and I'm losing you," I said, with sorrow.

"You haven't even met me yet. Your me, anyway."

"I don't know if he wants to meet, you saw how he turned red every time he looked at me. He's horrified by that video."

"Have a little faith, it's all good," Brian said, squeezing my elbow. "He has good taste. He is brilliant, after all. And you are beautiful and creative and kooky. It's an irresistible combination."

"How am I going to meet him for real? I'm so embarrassed about the video," I murmured. "How could I ever approach him?"

"You might not," Brian said with the disarming honesty that I'd come to love. He shrugged. "I don't know what choices you'll make here to create what universes. But in case you do, I have something for him." He gave me an envelope labeled PROFESSOR BRIAN TENNYSON. "This is for you." He handed me the wedding photo of him, Ofee, and me.

"Happiest day of my life," he said softly.

"I can't take this." I thrust it back at him. "It's your keepsake of your dead wife."

"I don't need it now, I have her in my heart. Besides, it may turn into slime in a few minutes." He stood up from the bench and shrugged, a giant, jovial gesture that was completely typical of him. "Not sure, cause it's not organic."

"Well, then, great, thank you. I love slime," I said. I blinked rapidly to keep tears from veiling my eyes. "I have something for you, too. Probably should have given it to you earlier." I held out a small wrapped package.

Brian tore it open and then exclaimed and chortled. "Superman undies! My favorite!" He hugged me.

"I hope they decohere back with you."

"Me too." He released me and pulled a folded-up paper from his pocket. "I hope this does, too." He unfolded one of my drawings. "I love this one where they're having a picnic. I can't wait to show it to Rajiv. He's my assistant back home."

"They're not—okay, they're having a picnic," I said. I tried again to restrain tears. "Just promise me you won't forget me. Not your Tessa, me."

Brian tilted my face up to look him in the eyes. "How could I? You're a wonderful, breathtaking Tessa Barnum. You're not the Tessa Barnum I married, but you're a perfect flowering of the Tessa Barnum seed that was planted and bloomed in this world."

I wanted to answer, but a deep hum sounded. A blue portal swirled open, like a door opening suddenly in space. It was filled with concentric rings like a pond after a rock is tossed in.

“Beam me up, Scotty!” Brian laughed. “I always wanted to say that.” He stepped into the shimmering blue portal and vanished.

The portal collapsed and the hum stopped abruptly.

I felt more empty, and at the same time, more full than I had ever felt in my life.

36 The sting

Looking mighty uncomfortable with his hair slicked back and a pencil mustache drawn on his face with mascara, Reverend Pincek wore a slinky black suit, compliments of Frances Gates.

My Fishnets friend from jail clung to his arm and cooed at him. She was playing her part as his girlfriend to repay me for her portrait. She was all over him like the smile on the Mona Lisa, but a lot less restrained.

The rev was white-lipped, and his face was covered with a fine sheen of perspiration, but he was doing his best to hold up his end of the charade.

I wondered if he'd ever had this much play in his whole life? It was too delicious, and I felt wicked for enjoying his discomfiture. I had to take a few surreptitious photos with my camera phone.

The two of them walked toward Rat Rock. Guy stood in his old place.

There were some words and gestures. The rev started nodding. Guy opened his bag. The rev held up his hands as if sermonizing.

A S.W.A.T. team erupted from behind trees, inside bushes, and under baby carriages to close in on Guy.

The look of surprise and horror on Guy's face was even better than if he'd succumbed to lung cancer.

I wished Brian was here to see it. I closed my eyes for a moment and sent him a loving thought, wherever he was in the multiverse.

37 The return of the king

A couple of detectives and a police officer, the guard, me, the rev, and Fishnets all stood in Frances Gates's gallery alongside two cameramen with reporters and a live-blogger filming the event with his iPad.

Frances replaced the skull on its pedestal, and we all applauded while he took a bow. We all clapped for the rev, who gave a queasy smile, when Gates pointed to him. Then Frances walked over and gestured at the Warholish nudes. Frances winked at me, a clownish, exaggerated thing.

Fishnets whistled with her thumb and forefinger between her lips. The rev stared, wide eyed.

"Well, Tessa, darling," Frances said. "I'm pleased. I am so happy that I've made a decision: I will buy your oil-on-eviction notice outright."

"Make the check out to the church," I said, immediately. "There's a leak that has to be fixed."

"Sure. I won't pay you much, and in a few years, when I've made your name, this'll be worth a fortune," Frances said affably. "It's all good."

"Wait," I said, holding up my hands. I gave the rev an apologetic look. "Make the check out to me. I have to take care of myself first. And pay my bills. Sorry, Rev."

"No need to apologize, Tessa," Reverend Pincek said. "You're not ready to be an angel yet. You're too alive for that. I guess none of us is quite ready to be beatified." He snuck a glance at Fishnets, who blew him a kiss from her Shanghai Red lips.

"It'll be a long time before I'm ready," I murmured.

"Amen!" The rev snuck a look at the Warholish paintings. "Frances here offered to curate a small show at the church and donate the proceeds."

"Just to thank you for your part in the sting that recovered Tessa's head and that she is allowing me to exhibit," Frances said.

"Well, I think I played a believable rascal," the rev said, modestly.

"Rev, you were a fabulous rascal," Frances said. "Keep the black suit, it looks smashing on you."

"I don't think so," the rev started.

Fishnets cut him off. "You can wear it to take me out. On the house, of course."

"I'm much too busy at the church," the rev said, dismayed.

Frances gestured for me to follow him to his office. I obeyed.

"Frances, despite the terrible art you show, you're a good guy," I said.

"Watch it, I'll be showing your art in a few months. And quit hugging me! What is it with you people?" he gargled.

Brian-like, I had wrapped myself around him, in gratitude.

38 The wedding photo

Reverend Pincek and I went from the gallery to the cemetery. Along the way, the rev scrubbed his face and changed his jacket. I stopped and bought a pair of racy, gold sling-back stilettos. The rev raised his eyebrows but didn't comment.

The funeral was a solemn affair with Mrs. Leibowitz's children and their spouses and children, some friends, and a bearded Rabbi who led us in Mourner's Kaddish.

I thought of all the times Mrs. L had made me laugh, how much I had enjoyed her over the last few years. I thought of her arch way of speaking and her kindness and her love for her Bernie. I was going to miss her. My heart ached with absence.

I pulled out the photo Brian had given me. It had changed. Brian and Ofee were gone. It was now a picture of me by myself, radiant in the white confection of the wedding dress. I had to smile through my tears. The future was open for me with all its possibilities.

That night I gave José a check for the co-op board. Then I turned my kitchen table into an easel stand. I set out my paints and brushes on the table. I threw an apron over my jeans and pulled on Mrs. L's fluffy turquoise slippers. I put the wedding photo up on my refrigerator door with a magnet, I saluted the Chagall on the wall, and I started painting for real.

39 An invitation

A few months later, just as the new college semester was starting, Ofee went with me to the Columbia campus, ostensibly to help me tape up fliers. He was really there to stand in tree pose while I attached the fliers to obliging posts and walls.

"This is pretty radical of you, Tessy," Ofee observed as he segued into bird of paradise pose. "I didn't know you had it in you. I like it."

"Anyone who signs up for my class will be lucky," I said. "I have a great passion about art to share." The fliers said ART AND LOVE: CLASSES IN LANDSCAPE PAINTING AND FIGURE DRAWING WITH NOTED ARTIST TESSA BARNUM, COLUMBIA GRADUATE. In the center of the flier was an image of the new painting I'd just completed, a mythical landscape featuring poignant, whimsical figures. On the bottom were tear-off strips with my cell number.

"I like that, 'noted,' even though it isn't completely true, yet," said Ofee. He moved easily into warrior three.

"Somewhere in the multiverse there's a world where I'm already a famous painter. I just have to choose that reality," I said. "My website will be up by next week."

We wended our way around Havemeyer, and I taped up more fliers while Ofee continued his practice. He did fifteen minutes of arm balances, and I chatted with some students about the class I was offering. Then I realized we stood smack in front of Pupin Hall, home of the physics department.

"Brian," I said. "I mean, Professor Brian Tennyson."

"Is that where his office is?" Ofee said.

"Yes, and I'm going to do this," I decided, just like that.

Ofee, bending backward in full wheel, grunted.

I laid the stack of papers on his belly and marched in to Pupin.

I stood outside a door marked DR. BRIAN TENNYSON. Peeking inside, I saw the stylish, well-groomed professor from the lecture. He was talking to a student but noticed me. He gave me a quirky, embarrassed glance and motioned me to come inside.

As he finished his conversation, I wandered around his office, examining mementoes and diplomas. A few shelves of his bookcase were filled with copies of his books. Another shelf held photos: Brian wearing a rock-climbing harness, clinging to a sheer granite rock face; Brian holding in his arms a decidedly ugly three-legged dog. There was a picture of an older couple who were probably his parents. No photos of a girlfriend.

"Hello there, can I help you?" asked Professor Tennyson as the student exited.

"Cute dog," I said.

Professor Tennyson walked over and took down the picture, gazing at it sentimentally. "That was Bella. Great girl, kooky, but sassy and spunky and fun. She passed away about a year ago. I still miss her."

"It takes time to heal from a loss," I murmured. I leaned a little closer and tried to sniff unobtrusively: did he smell like the other Brian?

"It does take time," Professor Tennyson said, his affect softening. "But why are you here? You're not one of my students coming in to grub for grades already."

Did he really not recognize me from the video? Maybe he was acting ignorant. If so, I could play along. "I'm Tessa Barnum. I'm an artist. We've never met, but I saw you a couple times a few months ago. I went to your lecture and then you came to a church dance."

"That's right, that crazy guy with the metric tensors phoned me and told me to go to the dance." He laughed. "I mean, I don't mean to insult him if he's a friend of yours. He seemed smart and interesting. A bit of a crackpot, though."

I had to smile. "Absotively, posilutely a crackpot. Well, I'd like to invite you to a show of my work." I handed him a postcard, which advertised: MANY WORLDS: LANDSCAPES OF POSSIBILITY. FORGERY, ART, AND A NEW OLD MASTER. TESSA BARNUM AT THE FRANCES GATES GALLERY."

On the postcard was a photo montage of the Bucknell skull, one of my landscapes, and some of my figure drawings. It was striking; Frances had designed it for maximum effect.

"The skull is ugly and kind of cheesy. I'm sorry, I know a lot of people like that stuff." He made a half-shrug of apology. "The figure drawings are beautiful. Reminds me of Bruegel. The old masters understood something important about life."

"You get it about art!" I cried involuntarily.

"I should, my mother was an illustrator, and she dragged me to every art museum in the world, insisting I take drawing lessons." He smiled. "Physics and art aren't so different in their search for the truth, I guess. What are the people doing, building a sand castle?"

"They're doing whatever you want them to be doing," I said, nodding.

"Cool."

"So, are you coming?" I asked.

He looked away and colored slightly. "I'm kind of busy with the new semester starting, and I have to finish up a paper for a colloquium . . . ."

"Sure." I dipped my head with understanding, though I was disappointed. "This is for you, too." From my messenger bag I pulled the envelope from the other Brian. I had carried it with me every day since he returned to his world.

"What's this?"

"Don't know," I said briskly. "I won't take up any more of your time. Thanks for seeing me." I went to the door. At the door I was literally struck by a thought. It seemed to come from outside myself—it seemed, if such a thing was possible, to come from the other Tessa. I could almost hear her silvery laugh fading away. I turned around and gave Professor Tennyson a wide-eyed look. "Hey, professor, did you hear that entropy isn't what it used to be?"

• • •

Ofee was nowhere in sight, which meant some college kids had corralled him into an impromptu yoga class. He'd be somewhere on the lawn demonstrating some impossible pose, wrapping his legs backwards around his head to close his eyelids with his toes, or something. I walked across campus looking for him.

Students strolled past, chattering. Around each of their heads, I imagined planets orbiting, planets filled with multiple landscapes and diverse groups of figures and branching paths. It was a rich, vibrant vision; maybe I would try my hand at painting it. Lately I was taking risks in my paintings. Not all the results were wonderful, but some turned out rather well.

Then I heard footsteps approaching me, sneakers slapping the pavement, and I had a flash of dêjà vu. I turned and it was Professor Tennyson running toward me. I felt a surge of challenge and joy. I took a deep breath and told myself, "Game on."

"Hey, do you know what this is?" the Professor demanded, panting. He thrust the letter in my face.

I shook my head no.

"It's a schematic for a many worlds device to travel across parallel universes."

"Cool," I mumbled.

He grabbed my shoulder. "*In my own handwriting!*"

"Interesting," I said and laughed.

"I came here from a parallel universe and gave it to you, didn't I? Didn't I!"

"Why would you think that?" I wondered.

"Because the letter says, 'Kiss the woman who brought this to you, and don't let go of her. You don't know what it will be like to lose her.'"

I was overtaken by an impulse. Almost without conscious volition, I leaned forward and kissed his lips gently. Then I stepped back. He looked incredulous. I opened my mouth to apologize, but then I thought, what would the other Brian tell me to do?

What had the girls advised: go for it?

So, I kissed him again.

After a moment, Brian pulled me into his body. After another minute, his mouth and hands answered me, passion for passion.

Tingling in all my girl parts, I wrested myself back from him. "I give you an A for that!"

"You'd better. Don't think I didn't recognize you from that video of us on the Internet," he said, his voice husky. "So I have a question. That was him, wasn't it? The other me. It has to be, because that was me in the video, and I'd remember something that awesome."

"Well . . . "

Smiling shyly, he put his hands on my hips and drew me in again. "I want a chance to star in my own video with you. I was good in that one, but I can do better."

"Just come to my show," I said.

Two weeks later, he did.

Acknowledgments

Many of Guy's lines are drawn from *History of Beauty*, edited by Umberto Eco. Translated by Alastair McEwen. (Rizzoli: New York, 2005).

Many thanks to Lori Handelman for brilliant editing and warm support, and to Drew Stevens for the ever ingenious book designs.

Thanks to Tammy Salyer for thoughtful copyediting.

Many thanks to Gerda and Mark Swearengen, Chris and Stuart Gartner, Michelle Czernin von Chudenitz, Jan Bröberg Carter, Dani Antman, Komilla Sutton, Don Steelman, Sarah Novotny, Lynn Bell, Dr. Dan Booth Cohen, and Mary T. Browne for the warm support. I love you all.

Many thanks to Sarah Miniaci for excellent PR. Thank you to Jarred Weisfeld and Meghan Kilduff for eBook support.

Many thanks to Kristin Gamble and Charlie Flood for being wizards.

Thank you to Dr. Bill Chambers, who has something to say about growing up.

Thank you to Adrienne Rosado, who keeps the faith.

Thank you to Scott Elrod for his early encouragement. Scott: you rock!

Warm thanks to Claudia and Steve Jackson, Teri and Steve Himes, and everyone at Telemachus Press for on-going support and encouragement.

Warm thanks to the readers and bloggers who have read and loved my novels and asked for more.

Love and thanks to Julia Howard, and to my indefatigable research assistant Madeleine Howard.

Thank you to my husband Sabin Howard, who has everything to say about art.

ABOUT THE AUTHOR

Traci L. Slatton is a graduate of Yale and Columbia. She lives in Manhattan and travels regularly to Italy, which inspired her historical novel *Immortal* and her contemporary art history mystery *The Botticelli Affair*. Her romantic dystopian After Trilogy is made up of *Fallen*, *Cold Light*, and *Far Shore*. *The Love of My (Other) Life* is a bittersweet romantic comedy. *The Art of Life* is a photo essay about figurative sculpture, and *Dancing In the Tabernacle* is her first book of poetry.

www.ingramcontent.com/pod-product-compliance
Lightning Source LLC
LaVergne TN
LVHW010055110826
845155LV00028B/358

* 9 7 8 1 9 4 2 5 2 3 0 8 6 *